The Spirit of the Samurai

 New Generation Publishing

Foreword

The ultimate warrior of Japan came to power with Japan's first *shogun*, Minamoto Yoritomo, and the creation of the Kamakura military government, *bakufu*, in 1185. This warrior was known as *bushi* and, although they prevailed throughout the feudal era (1185-1868), the Kamakura *bushi* were in a different league, ethically, morally and in fighting prowess, from the *bushi* of later years, and were directly behind the development of the classical martial arts, *bujutsu*, and the revered code of conduct, *bushido*. At the heart of their training lay the *zen* method and it was well known that the quality of technical performance depended on the mind of the practitioner and that spiritual power was the essence of mastery.

When the Tokugawa era (1603-1868) ended the feudal period was over and the new government was controlled by the *samurai*. In the fifteenth century, the term *samurai* described a category of *bushi*, but not the highest, and in the Tokugawa era there were different ranks within the *samurai* class. After 1868 the term *samurai* became synonymous with *bushi*, the professional warrior, and were those allowed to wear the *daisho*, the long and short swords.

Chapter 1

Commander Ruth Arnall of the Specialist Crime Directorate, New Scotland Yard, closed the door and went to her desk, lifting the telephone as she sat down. It was nine in the morning and cold. She glanced at the pad as she dialled a number in Pretoria. Bruce Weisz, head of regional South Africa's Directorate for Priority Crime Investigation, the DPCI or Hawks, formerly the Directorate: Special Operations, the DSO or Scorpions, answered.

'Bruce, Ruth Arnall, Scotland Yard. We met a couple of years ago in London.'

'Yes,' said Weisz. 'I remember meeting you. I heard you were Adam Fairley's boss before he joined us. You know he was killed?'

'Yes,' said Arnall. 'I was very sorry to hear about it. He was an able officer and going high in the Met before he joined you in the Republic. He was shot in his flat by one of your agents?'

'Yes,' said Weisz. 'He was investigating a plan to replace four cabinet ministers by men connected to organized crime. Unfortunately the ministers were killed before we caught the guys behind it. Do you know anything about the case?'

'Only what I read in the press,' said Ruth. 'I knew his death was linked to the case and I followed the trial of the men convicted with interest. This is the reason for my call. Do you have a few minutes?'

'I'm listening,' said Weisz. 'It's serious?'

'It involves the murder of Brit Enoksen a Swedish girl in Hyde Park,' said Arnall. 'I want to arrest the person who did it. We believe we know who it is but it's a case of getting hold of him. The girl was found early yesterday morning by a park attendant.'

'The guy's probably fled the country, gone into hiding or both,' said Weisz.

'He's left the UK and we know where he's gone,' said Arnall. 'We also know where we can find him. The problem is how to bring him back here.'

'Now you've got me going,' said Weisz. 'Where do I come in? You're going to tell me he's in South Africa.'

'He's a Japanese national and now in Japan,' said Arnall. 'That's where I think you can help me. After Adam Fairley left the Met he kept in touch with some of us here. A few days before his death, I spoke to him on the phone. He said he was involved in the case involving the ministers and that he was on it with an Englishman who had been pulled in to help. He wondered if I'd heard of him because he had been brought over from London on a one-off basis. The guy lives here and had apparently been involved in DSO work before. Adam was simply curious. He gave me the man's name. I didn't see his name mentioned during the trials, not that I was looking for it at the time.'

'You're talking about James Steiner,' said Weisz. 'The only agents of mine mentioned at the trials were those killed, including Fairley, and Conran, who was on the wrong side and convicted. We don't reveal names unless it is necessary.'

'So Steiner played no real part in the arrests?' said Arnall.

'I'm not saying that,' said Weisz. 'He played a very important part, but he was not required to appear. The evidence spoke for it itself and the men were convicted. Why are you interested in Steiner? What's he got to do with this call?'

'I said earlier that it might not be easy to bring our

suspect back to the UK,' said Arnall. 'Only the USA and South Korea have extradition treaties with Japan. Even if we had a treaty and compelling evidence of guilt a person would not be extradited if, as in this case, they are a Japanese national. We are having this confirmed. If it is negative it means bringing the person out not only against their will but illegally, or, shall I say, under cover without the Japanese knowing. The suspect is a powerful political figure in Japan with extensive business interests. The job of snatching him and removing him in secret would require someone with specific attributes. Perhaps the most significant of these are knowledge of Japan and the Japanese, and the ability to operate calmly against strong opposition. The suspect is also the Japanese prime minister's only nephew, and, as he has no sons, it means a lot in that country. From what Adam Fairley told me during our brief conversation, Steiner has those qualities. Japan is a very different place from here and I believe that would be a distinct advantage. I hear Steiner also successfully carried out two complex jobs for the DSO before being brought in on the last job?'

'Yes,' said Weisz. 'The first two were through our Durban office and the man who took him on, Peter Smith, was killed by one of the men involved in the last job.'

'I didn't know that,' said Ruth. 'I presume he was killed by one of the men convicted.'

'No,' said Weisz. 'Smith's killer was killed and this was not a part of the trial.'

'Did one of your men do it?' asked Ruth.

'Yes,' said Weisz, 'but we digress. Steiner's assignment was a one-off as you said but he did it with some reluctance. He had become a good friend of Smith's. I was short of the type of man I needed and persuaded Smith to ask him. I doubt Steiner would want the Japan job. The work over here was conducted inside the law, and going in and pulling out another country's citizen without authorisation is politically very dangerous, especially when the country is as powerful as Japan. That doesn't mean I wouldn't do what you're thinking of doing, but I wouldn't like it. I'm surprised you haven't got your own men who can undertake this work. What about one of the other agencies?'

'We don't have someone who could act independently - which we'd like since we don't want direct association - and has the credentials I mentioned,' said Ruth. 'We are also reluctant to involve other agencies in something like this. It won't be a case of just walking in and removing the suspect. We have run checks on him and he has two places of residence. His main one is a traditional Japanese estate five hours north-west of Tokyo in the mountainous region of Oku-Nikko. He's a renowned collector of artefacts from Japan's Edo period, the time when the Tokugawa *shoguns* ruled.'

'That doesn't mean getting him will be difficult,' said Weisz dryly.

'The person who goes to find the suspect will be told everything we know,' said Arnall. 'I'll leave it at that but Steiner's particular type of training might come in useful.'

'I don't like what I'm hearing,' said Weisz. 'Steiner came up against some pretty nasty people out here and dealt with them by taking appropriate action. He has no formal training as an agent.'

'That's what I mean,' said Ruth ambiguously. 'Formal training as an agent does not necessarily get results. In some cases a developed intuition is invaluable and Steiner would have acquired that during his extensive *karatedo* training in Japan. It's the essence of mastery in that and similar *budo* arts such as *aikido*. If you give me his number in London, he will be told everything we know.'

'How is the suspect connected politically?' said Weisz.

'He is a member of the ruling Liberal Democratic Party and a cabinet minister, minister of state for economy, trade and industry,' said Arnall bluntly. 'He is seen as a future prime minister of Japan.'

'That's strong enough reason for the Japanese not to want to extradite him,' said Weisz.

'Yes,' said Ruth, 'but we have given the Japanese authorities his name and the evidence, and before we decide to send someone in we want to know where we stand. We're preparing ourselves for a refusal.' She stood up. 'The killer must be brought to trial.'

Weisz was interested but knew there was nothing more she would tell him. 'I'll phone Steiner, tell him what you've told me and get his response,' he said. 'I'll get back to you.'

'Thank you,' said Ruth. 'We'd like to move as soon as possible.'

Chapter 2

Knightsbridge, London SW7

James Steiner was at home, a mews house in Knightsbridge, when he received the telephone call from Bruce Weisz. It was eleven-thirty in the morning. 'Bruce, I hope this is not another offer of work.'

Weisz was at his desk. He liked Steiner. 'We miss you down here. All that excitement wound me up. I started enjoying my job. It seems like yesterday.'

'I don't miss it,' said Steiner. 'Thank you for all the stuff you sent me during the trials. It made different reading from what I got in the press. The sentences didn't surprise me.'

'It is what they deserved,' said Weisz. 'James, I've just had a phone call from Commander Ruth Arnall of New Scotland Yard. I met her once when I was in London. She was Adam Fairley's boss in the Met before he joined the Scorpions.'

Steiner looked across the room at his girlfriend, Kirsty Callard, seated on a sofa. He nodded his head slowly. Something was coming that would involve him. 'Why are you telling me?'

'I'm coming to that,' said Weisz. 'When Adam was assigned to the ministers' case he mentioned you and told her about your training in Japan. It seems to have impressed her. A few days ago a Swedish girl was murdered in Hyde Park and the suspect is a high profile Japanese male.' He relayed details of Kitamura as given to him by Ruth. 'Arnall wants to get him out. That's where you come in.'

'Now I've heard everything,' said Steiner. 'What does she think I am? She doesn't know me, and simply living in Japan is hardly a serious asset. Surely with the right evidence the British can have him extradited.'

'That's the problem,' said Weisz, wondering why he had suddenly become a go-between. 'There is no extradition treaty with Japan, and even if there was, the man is a Japanese national. I also suspect the evidence might not be as good as they'd like.'

'I still can't believe this,' said Steiner. 'She wants me to go to Japan, grab this guy when no one is looking and pull him out of the country?'

'Something along those lines,' said Weisz, amused. 'I'm afraid I can't help you with the details. All she wanted from me was your phone number so she can contact you. It's not as you think.'

'I'm going by what you told me,' said Steiner. 'Did you give her my number?'

'No,' said Weisz. 'I wanted to phone you first. She's a very nice woman and I would like you to hear what she's got to say. Even if you won't help her, there might be something you can suggest.'

'I'm not a diplomat,' said Steiner. 'She should be speaking to the foreign office.'

'She's doing that, but she's also looking at a possible alternative in case things don't work out,' said Weisz. 'If you like, I'll tell her you're not interested. She'll be very disappointed. I get the feeling she's not doing this purely for professional reasons.'

'You're saying it's personal,' said Steiner. 'What gives you that impression?'

'Forget I said that,' said Weisz. 'I'm probably wrong. What do you want me to tell her?'

'She can phone me. I'll tell her what I've told you,' said Steiner.

'Thank you,' said Weisz. 'I'll ring her now. I'd like to hear from you after she makes contact.'

'I'll phone you,' said Steiner.

When Weisz had gone, Steiner returned to Kirsty. 'You guessed that was Bruce Weisz.'

'He's the only Bruce you know,' said Kirsty. 'He has another job for you. Surely the DSO has men down there.'

'You're right,' said Steiner. 'It is a job but not down there and not for the DSO.' He told her what Weisz had said. 'He obviously likes the woman and wants me to hear her out. He'll give her this number.'

'I know you,' she said. 'You're interested. If you weren't you'd have said no. The thought of you going to Japan to kidnap a prominent Japanese politician suspected of murder is bizarre. MI6 does that sort of thing and when they screw up all hell breaks loose. You don't have that sort of training. Who do they think you are?'

'Someone good enough to do their hard work,' he said. 'I admit I'm a little interested. Perhaps I just like going after people like that.'

'I don't believe you,' said Callard. 'You would never have done the work for the DSO if you hadn't believed the criminal activities of those guys had to be ended.' She went quiet, wondering if what he had said had some truth and he had come to like the excitement of chasing those wanted by the law. Steiner had clearly enjoyed police work but for what reason? She had never asked, and in his case he seemed to have taken a liking to being involved with those on the other side. What were her real feelings after her own experiences? She looked at him. 'When will she ring?'

'Bruce will phone her,' said Steiner. 'Don't worry I'm not about to jump into anything I don't like. Let's go out for something to eat.'

Chapter 3

New Scotland Yard, London SW1

Ruth Arnall received the call from Weisz at noon. 'Bruce. You've spoken to him?'

'Yes,' said Weisz. 'He's not interested but is prepared to speak to you. I don't know him all that well, but if you really want him, a little persuasion might pull him in.'

'I'll try him now,' said Ruth. 'I won't tell him anything over the phone. I have to meet him. There's something fascinating about him. I'll let you know what he says.'

After the call, Ruth waited a few minutes and then rang Steiner's number. He answered.

'James Steiner, Ruth Arnall. I believe Bruce Weisz told you I'd phone.'

'Yes,' said Steiner. 'He called earlier and said you're looking for someone to go to Japan. From what he told me I'm not the type you want.'

'I think you are,' said Ruth. 'You've already excelled in work that could be similar to what I'd like you to do for us. I can't give you the details over the phone. I'd like to meet you. You might be interested enough to go. You would be rewarded.'

'Where would you like to meet?' said Steiner.

'You live in Knightsbridge,' said Arnall. 'There's a pub called the Bunch of Grapes opposite the entrance to the Holy Trinity Church on the Brompton Road. How about meeting there at six this evening? I'll be in a red dress. I'm in my thirties and have dark hair.'

'I'll see you then,' said Steiner.

Chapter 4

Knightsbridge, London SW7

Steiner reached the Bunch of Grapes, a little before six, and found a table with views of the front and side entrances. There were only a few people in the place.

At five past six, he saw a woman enter, dressed in red. She looked to be in her late thirties. As Steiner got to his feet, the woman walked towards him.

'James Steiner?' she said as she neared him. 'Ruth Arnall.'

'I'm Steiner,' he said, showing her to a seat at the table. She was very attractive with a striking figure. 'May I get you a drink?'

'Anything soft,' she said, sitting down. Steiner went to the bar and returned with two drinks.

'I'm glad you came,' said Arnall, taking a sip from her glass. 'After talking to Bruce I didn't think you'd agree to a meeting.'

'He's a friend,' said Steiner, 'and I'm a little curious. It's not straight forward.'

'It was a particularly savage killing,' said Arnall. 'Her name was Brit Enoksen, twenty-three, an English student at a school near Regent's Park. She had only been here for two months and the new term had just started.'

'Why would someone want to kill her?' said Steiner.

'That's what I intend to find out,' said Arnall, 'but it will mean bringing the person in. What we've got points to the Japanese minister.'

'We don't have an extradition treaty with Japan and he's a Japanese national,' said Steiner. 'You want someone to pull him out and you thought of me.'

'Yes,' said Arnall. 'At the moment we're speaking

to the Japanese authorities, but our chances of getting him legally aren't good. That's why we'll probably have to go and get him. A classic example was Alberto Fujimoro, ex-president of Peru. He was apparently very successful, but made enemies. When the heat got too great he fled to Japan. Extradition to Peru, even in the face of damning evidence, was denied because he was a Japanese national. Unfortunately for him he paid a visit to Chile to resurrect his political career. The Chileans nabbed him and he was finally extradited. He now awaits trial.' She drank some juice. 'No one will go for Kitamura until we're sure, but let me tell you what happened and what we know.' She looked at him closely. 'Four nights ago, Brit Enoksen was having a drink with some friends in the Whisky Malt club at the Hilton Hotel on Park Lane. It is one of the in-places and very popular with those who are loaded, particularly the spoilt young who have very rich parents.'

'And she was one of them?' said Steiner.

'She had very wealthy parents but was not spoilt,' said Arnall. 'While Brit and her two Swedish girlfriends were at the club, the Japanese man entered. It was around ten. His name is Shingen Kitamura and he was with a younger European male. They approached the table where the girls were sitting. Kitamura was attracted to Brit, and they danced and spoke at length. After an hour the other man left, and a little later Kitamura left with Brit. That's the last her friends saw of her. She was found dead at five-thirty the next morning in Hyde Park by a park attendant. She'd been stabbed in the chest, her throat slit, and was covered in blood. It was a violent killing, the work of a crazed killer.'

Steiner was still, his eyes on Ruth. 'When were you notified? How was she identified?'

'The police were there ten minutes after she was found,' said Arnall. 'The attendant called us on his mobile. She had no identification on her, but her flatmate called the police. She was worried because Brit had phoned her soon after leaving the Dorchester Hotel, where she'd apparently gone. Brit's words were: "I'm glad to get out of there. He's a pervert. I'm getting a cab." The girl said Brit didn't return before she went to bed, and she became alarmed when Brit did not show for lectures at the language school. She and another girl identified the body and gave us some of Brit's personal items, including her passport and contacts here and overseas.'

'How do you know she was not spoilt?' said Steiner.

'You're clever,' said Arnall. 'I didn't see her until after she'd been identified but when I did I recognised her. A few years ago I was in Voss, a Norwegian skiing resort. Brit and members of her family, including her father and mother, were staying at the same hotel. We met and became friends. I knew Brit was coming to London at some stage but didn't know she was already here. Her parents told me she planned to make contact with me. They are devastated.'

'And your friendship with the family is one of the reasons you are so keen to get the killer,' said Steiner. 'As I understand it, you haven't exhausted the normal channels of getting hold of him. Does your boss know all this and your plan to bring him back?'

'Yes, Assistant Commissioner Craig Holden,' said Arnall without hesitation. 'I admit that knowing the girl increases my desire to get the person who did it.'

'What points to Kitamura as the killer?' said Steiner.

Arnall couldn't help being attracted to Steiner, his smooth, handsome features and blue-green eyes. She wondered if there was a woman in his life. 'As soon as we arrived on the scene, a search was made of the area. An unusual folding stiletto with a locking blade was found in a bin a few hundred metres from the body. It had traces of Brit's blood on it and no fingerprints. The knife is made by the German company Puma and not readily available. You will seldom find it in stores that stock the usual Swiss Army and other folding knives and there are not many of those about. Also, this one is a specific design in the range, a Medici stiletto, and is still harder to find. After a few hours we found one stockist in London, in the Burlington Arcade off Piccadilly. The manager told us that an identical knife had been bought there two days before the killing. The man was Japanese and paid in cash.'

'What else is there?' said Steiner. He finished his drink. 'You know how to hold my interest.'

'How else am I going to get you?' said Arnall. 'The next break came from Brit's friends. They remembered Kitamura saying he was staying at the Dorchester and when he and Brit left, Brit said they were going there. We spoke to the Dorchester and a female receptionist remembers them coming in at eleven. Kitamura has stayed at the hotel before. The receptionist was also on duty when Brit left an hour later on her own. A few minutes later Kitamura appeared in the lobby and also left the hotel. He returned some forty-five minutes later and went to his room. At five-thirty the next morning he checked out of the hotel. He was returning to Japan, flying in his private jet from general aviation at Heathrow. We confirmed that later.'

'Let me get you another drink,' said Steiner, picking up his glass and reaching for hers. She accepted and he returned shortly afterwards with two more drinks. 'Please go on,' he said when he was seated. 'You haven't told me what else you've got on this guy.'

'A post-mortem revealed that she'd had sexual

intercourse earlier,' said Arnall. 'We have DNA from the semen found in her but don't have his DNA and can't make a match. It's likely they had sex in his bedroom. When we found her, her knickers and tights were firmly in place and there was no forced entry.'

'It sounds as if he wanted more and she didn't,' said Steiner. 'Everything you've told me points to him, but it isn't enough, including the possibility that he was the man who bought the knife. It's all circumstantial and even if the DNA from the semen matched Kitamura's, it doesn't mean he killed her. Neither would he be convicted if his DNA or fingerprints were found on the knife.'

'There is more,' said Arnall. 'An elongated, amorphous blood stain the size of a pound coin was found on the blade of the knife. It was not there before the killing since it overlapped some of Brit's blood. We believe the blood stain belongs to Kitamura but again we don't have his DNA and can't make a match. The hard evidence we want rests on finding him and getting a sample. But we recognize that even with a perfect match we still have to bring him back for prosecution and it would have to be done illegally because of the extradition problem.'

'A DNA match on the blood stain would certainly give you the evidence,' said Steiner, 'and with what you've described would get a conviction. But you have to get him and you'd be taking a massive risk bringing a leading Japanese citizen, the prime minister's nephew, a member of the cabinet and a possible future prime minister, back here against his will. Even if you're successful in bringing him back, how'd you explain it? What if his DNA doesn't match that yielded by the blade. He and his lawyers would go crazy and bring you all down. The political fallout would be nuclear and reach the top of both governments, dragging in both prime ministers. I'd also be locked up as the one who'd gone and got him.'

'We will deal with that when the time comes,' said Arnall. 'We don't intend to reveal anything and go for prosecution until all the evidence is there.' She stared at him. 'At some stage before he is jumped we might decide to call the whole thing off but a lot depends on what you find when you get there.'

'Who else besides Craig Holden knows about your plan?' said Steiner. 'What about the Met commissioner?'

'The Met commissioner will be told when it's necessary and everything is lined up,' said Arnall. 'There's no reason to put him in the loop. Three other officers know. They are involved in the case and right behind me. I'll introduce you to them if you accept the job. They are members of my command, DCS Clive Dance, DS Gary Mercer and DI Jane Easter. They're very competent officers and, according to some, Dance will one day be the Met commissioner, head of Britain's police. Mercer is very ambitious and hard but perhaps things aren't going fast enough for him. I suspect Easter is sleeping with him but that's their business if they want to keep it quiet. She is very clever and will reach my rank. Do you know the police ranks and levels of seniority?'

'Anyone who turns on the TV knows them,' said Steiner. 'Whose idea was it to go to Japan?'

'Mine,' said Arnall. 'I believed it was the only way. We lost out on a similar case involving the son of a powerful businessman in Yemen and a murdered girl. She was also a student in London. We wanted the boy returned when things pointed to him but lost out for the same reason; no extradition treaty, a national, and a shortage of hard evidence. They wouldn't even send him back for questioning or allow our officers to visit him in Yemen. I don't want that to happen again.'

'If I caught this man, how would I get him out,' said Steiner. 'I hope you don't expect me to use a regular flight.'

'You do have a sense of humour,' said Arnall, 'but others have done it. The Israelis with the German Nazi Adolf Eichmann is an example. It was a big risk but several guys were involved in the planning and execution. In your case a private flight will be arranged to get you out but I'll fill you in on the details and your contacts in Japan when and if you accept the job.'

'Who are the contacts?' said Steiner. 'They can only be enemies of this guy.'

'Enemies of his would probably be enemies of ours,' said Arnall. 'Your main contact will be a senior officer in the Japanese police but his help will be limited. He'll simply give you some necessary details. That's all you need to know at this stage. Does anyone else know you're seeing me and have an idea what it's about?'

'I told my girlfriend when Weisz called,' said Steiner. 'She knows I'm seeing you but no one else. I wouldn't speak to others about this unless they were directly involved. I trust her and before I take it I'd want to discuss it with her.'

'Then it will stay in the family,' said Arnall. 'Kitamura knows we want to speak to him over here and will know we have little chance of getting him legally. The thing we don't want him to know is that we intend to get him; surprise is important. He is already well protected because of his position in politics. We noted with interest that when he left he was accompanied by three men, David Tate and Carl Norman, both British, and a Japanese, Shuji Oda. They are in their mid-thirties and didn't look like your usual businessman. They looked too healthy. We're checking them out but so far they're clean.' She shifted in her seat. 'You haven't said anything about money. Did the South Africans pay you?'

'It came in the end,' said Steiner. 'What are you prepared to pay? You must have a figure in mind.'

'My salary equivalent for days on the job,' said Arnall, unequivocally. 'I'm on over a hundred grand a year. You'll get expenses. How does that sound?'

'It's not a fortune,' said Steiner, 'but I'm more interested in getting the result. It will be over quickly.'

'I will give you until first thing in the morning for an answer,' said Arnall. 'We'll take it from there.'

'I'll ring you,' said Steiner, getting to his feet. 'Thank you.'

Chapter 5

Knightsbridge, London SW7

'What a way to die,' said Callard. 'I hope they bring the killer in.' She stared at him. 'The money's not bad but do you want to get involved? You have no real experience of this kind of work.' She and Steiner were seated in the lounge of their home. He had relayed his conversation with Ruth Arnall.

'I had no experience when I took on the DSO,' said Steiner, 'and what is the right type of experience? All these jobs are different and it gets down to whether or not you can deal with what turns up. Perhaps jobs like those in the Republic and this one were meant to come my way.'

'You haven't answered my question,' said Callard. 'Do you want to get involved?'

'Yes,' said Steiner. 'I'm being drawn to it.'

'Like a moth to the flame,' said Callard, reaching out and taking hold of his hand.

'I wouldn't put it like that,' said Steiner. 'What do you think? I told Arnall I'd talk to you first.'

'Did you find her attractive?' said Callard.

'What's that got to do with it?' said Steiner. 'She is very attractive but that's where it ends. No other woman excites me as you do. Why cross the street for silver when I've got gold at home.'

She kissed him. 'I won't try and dissuade you if that's what you feel you should do,' she said. 'I don't like the absence of evidence. You will be exposed from the very beginning when you try to get a sample of his DNA. You'll have to be sure it's his and get help from Arnall's police friend to see if there's a match. If the sample you get belongs to someone else, like one of those men on the plane, you'll look pretty stupid when a sample is taken from Kitamura in this country. Something in me says the three were associated with him, even if it was not obvious to the person or people the police spoke to at the airport. If you bring him back and he's found to be innocent, Arnall, her boss and others who knew about it will be right in it, including you. I'm sure you realise you won't know the danger until you get involved but the man has to be brought in if guilty and there is no one better than you to do it. I think you should go. I'll miss the training you've subjected to me since leaving the Republic but I'll get by.'

'You'll soon be at a stage when you don't need me,' said Steiner. 'The coordinated mind and body strength you've developed is already up there with some of the best I've met and confirms to me that some people learn more in a year than others in ten. It also depends on how you're taught. Your development is a direct result of the centralised breathing exercises and the meditations. They condition the intuition, the unconscious mind or the *zen* mind. The power behind your kicks and strikes on the heavy bag would drop anyone. They are very simple but for the old teachers, mastery of a few basic moves is what it is all about; there's no time for film antics or elaborate choreography in a real fight. I'll phone Ruth Arnall in the morning and tell her. She'll want me to see the other three officers involved in the case.'

Chapter 6

Pollsmoor High-Security Prison, Cape Town

Andrew Rohm's second term in Pollsmoor high-security prison was to him harder and more debilitating than the first. It was not the physical aspects that lowered his spirits, but the psychological, and, above all, he regretted being caught and returned when he was out of the country. His first arrest was for being associated with three men, John Conran, Paul Bale and Bryan Jones, who had killed four South African government ministers, and the second related to two young women, Kirsty Callard and Sophie Carswell. Callard had sighted him in central London and notified Bruce Weisz of what had been the Directorate of Special Operations, the Scorpions, and Carswell had recognized him when he had fled from London and bought a farm near the Kruger Reserve from Sophie's father, Jonathan Carswell. The chances of escaping from Pollsmoor and not being caught were virtually zero. It was in the Cape Town suburb of Tokai, close to the wealth of Constantia and the low slopes of Constantiaberg.

Late one afternoon Rohm was told by a guard that his lawyer, Harry Fisher, wanted to see him. Aside from being guilty of the murder of the ministers, Rohm was constantly being investigated for committing other crimes, in the past and while in prison. Those committed when a free man were his main concern; they were by far the more serious and could lead to further substantial sentences, which would prevent any form of leniency in the future. A time was arranged and the two men met in a private meeting room at nine the next morning.

'It's really good to see you again,' said Rohm when

they were seated. 'I hope you at least have some good news.'

'The news is not good,' said Fisher. 'You are under suspicion for shipping vast quantities of heroin from Afghanistan to Europe. There is a preliminary hearing coming up with prosecution soon afterwards. This is so serious you might never get out of this place. You know the difficulty of that.'

The two girls, Carswell and Callard, had effectively nailed him. If they hadn't seen him, all those thousands of miles away, he would still be free. He had used his men to make a hit on the car taking him to the court cells. A job like that was not pulled off every day.

Fisher seemed to know what Rohm was thinking. 'Why don't you vary the approach you take to get out, and then fly straight to London. There are BA and SAA flights at around six every evening to Heathrow.'

'You're not being clear,' said Rohm. 'How do I get to the airport? I appreciate that I'd have to go in a police car but I don't want to go through a hit again. It is too dangerous.'

'Last time you suggested paying the two police guards to make a detour but you changed your mind. You didn't involve them and used your own men to attack the car and free you.'

'That's right,' said Rohm.

'Well I think you should revert to your first suggestion,' said Fisher. 'By that I mean don't use your men to make a hit on the car. Simply pay the two police guards enough to drive you directly to the airport. And you can forget about the police placing cars at intervals along the route. They will not expect a hit as before. Neither will you have to stop off at a hotel to dye your hair; just wear dark glasses and a hat.'

'What about the other stuff and a change of identity?' said Rohm.

'I think the name Ray Malan will be suitable with the previous date and place of birth, 7 August 1963 and Whitechapel, British and South African passports, driving licences for the UK and RSA, birth certificate, credit cards, cash, and details of new bank accounts in the UK. I'll give you all this at the airport including hand luggage and a set of clothes for the hold. You'll be met at Heathrow by a guy with the usual board and taken to the Grosvenor House Hotel off Park Lane.'

'What about the guards?' said Rohm. 'They'll have to be brought in on the act.'

'I'll see that's done,' said Fisher, 'and they'll be well rewarded. You will fly tomorrow evening and we should meet two to three hours before. The first class lounge is perfect. I'll see you at the airport.'

The two men parted, and, the following afternoon, met in the first class lounge.

'This brief case contains all the documents we spoke about,' said Fisher. 'I wish you luck.'

Chapter 7

New Scotland Yard, London SW1

Ruth Arnall lifted the phone on the desk. 'Arnall.'

'Commander, James Steiner, I said I'd phone you about the job. I'd like to come and see you.'

Arnall swivelled in her seat and looked out of the window, smiling faintly. It was eight in the morning and she was at her desk in New Scotland Yard. 'Can you make it at nine?' she said. 'I've got something to clear first. Do you know where we are?'

'Broadway, SW1,' said Steiner. 'I'll be there then and ask for you at the desk.'

At a little before nine Steiner arrived at the Met's headquarters and met Arnall in the reception room.

'We can talk in the interview room,' said Arnall, pointing down the passage and leading the way. 'The officers I mentioned are waiting for us. They're looking forward to meeting you. I assume you are prepared to accept the assignment.'

'Yes,' said Steiner, 'unless I hear something that changes my mind.'

'I don't think you will. You're the type who can easily adapt, like the Japanese willow bending in the wind.'

'I'm not sure about that but I've been trying,' said Steiner tersely.

They reached the room and entered. It was utilitarian, sparsely furnished, and two men and a woman were seated around a large central table. They stood and waited for Ruth, moving to one side: 'Detective Chief Superintendent Clive Dance, Detective Superintendent Gary Mercer and Detective Inspector Jane Easter.' She nodded to each as she gave their names and then looked at Steiner. 'Please meet

James Steiner.'

Steiner stepped forward and gave his name as he shook each of their hands. He faced Arnall when he had finished.

She walked to a seat and indicated the one next to her for Steiner. When everyone was seated she said: 'James has informed me that he'll go to Japan. I've told him as much as we know about this end of the case and he'd like to hear from you. But it's the Japanese side we need to focus on so that we can start moving as soon as we hear from our people that getting Shingen Kitamura is formally and legally denied.'

'That's dead,' said Mercer. 'I heard from them earlier, after I last spoke to you. It is what we expected. The other issue against us is the man's status in Japan. He is forty-five, already a cabinet minister as minister of state for economy, trade and industry, and a highly regarded politician. He is also the only nephew of the Japanese prime minister, a man who has no son. When he is a little older it's almost a certainty he'll win the Liberal Democratic nomination for leader. The LDP is the governing party in the Diet since it has the majority in the lower house, the House of Representatives, and it has been in power since 1955. It recently had its new leader, a man in his late fifties, appointed prime minister after a general election which the upper house, the House of Counsellors and held by the Democratic Party of Japan, wanted. If the status quo continues and Kitamura becomes leader of the LDP he will be the next prime minister. He is not in this position without very powerful friends, colleagues in high places and advisers, and they would not entertain any suggestion that he is guilty of any particular crime, particularly this one, the murder of a young Swedish woman. According to our source in Tokyo, Kitamura also has or had strong links with the *yakuza*, the Japanese mafia, even though there is no evidence of such involvement. In recent years the *yakuza* has become even more dominant with their expansion of drugs, primarily amphetamines, gambling and prostitution, into financial crime. Friends like that make Kitamura virtually untouchable.'

Ruth looked at Steiner. 'There you have it,' she said. 'The door is open.'

'It sounds closed to me,' said Steiner. 'Now you're going to tell me he is guarded by the military.'

'That might be closer to the truth than you think,' said Mercer. 'Apparently Kitamura is the principal of a clandestine martial arts school. It is near his main country residence in the Oku-Nikko area north-west of Tokyo.'

Arnall interrupted. 'I don't give that a lot of credence,' she said to Steiner. 'Shimada's imagination is running wild. These schools and clubs are well regulated. The days of secrecy died with the end of the feudal period in 1868.'

'Who's Shimada?' said Steiner, briefly thinking of the two ninja he'd killed previously in a forest near Takayama, a remote, mountain village in Japan. They had come for him in the early hours of the morning.

'He's your contact,' said Arnall, 'and a Japanese police officer in Tokyo. We'll come to him. Clive, please carry on.'

'That's where I'll start,' said Dance. 'The Japanese police force is the National Police Agency or NPA and the head is the commissioner general. The Met equivalent in Japan is the Metropolitan Police Department of Tokyo and it's in the same building as the NPA. The head of the MPD is the *keishi-sokan*, the superintendent general. We haven't had any contact with him and we're unlikely to. On paper he is the boss of your contact, Kenichi Shimada, a superintendent supervisor or *keishi-kan*. We think Shimada has a deputy and Shimada's boss probably knows but he hasn't confirmed or denied this. That suits us and he can't be completely alone. As far as we are concerned, Shimada is the only one over there who knows we are going to try and get Kitamura.'

'And if I get hold of Kitamura,' said Steiner, 'it will appear Shimada was involved.'

'He will not be directly involved and it will be impossible to prove,' said Arnall. 'Shimada will only give you as much information as he dares to help you deliver the goods. There will be no physical backup or support from him. You will in effect be on your own and he'll ignore knowledge of your existence.'

'Let me be precise on this,' said Steiner. 'The only reliable way of comparing a DNA sample from Kitamara with the DNA on the knife is to get it from him physically, like a buccal swab. A sample from any other source such as a hair brush thought to be Kitamura's could be claimed as coming from someone else and not genuine. In reality that means bringing Kitamura back here. When he's here you'll be hoping to get a perfect match. This would remove some of the heat from bringing him back illegally and allow you to keep your jobs with some credit. If you don't get a perfect match and the Japanese find out he is here, you'll be in deep shit, and if you don't get a confession or other form of hard evidence quickly they'll go crazy. They'll want revenge and accountability at the highest level. How will you deal with that?'

'We'll deal with that if it arises,' said Arnall. 'We believe he is guilty and that we'll get what we want from him. Sometimes we have to take calculated risks to get to the truth.'

'How do I get out of Japan?' said Steiner. 'I'll need help from someone.'

'We've already organized that,' said Arnall.

'There'll be a business jet, a Learjet 45 XR, at your disposal. You can be out in hours through general aviation. When you're ready, ring me and I'll see the plane is waiting for you. Shimada won't be involved.' She looked at Dance. 'Please continue.'

'You will fly to Tokyo on a scheduled flight, BA or JAL, and carry a 90-day tourist visa,' said Dance. 'We'll book you in at the Hyatt Regency Hotel, Shinjuku. Shimada will be expecting you to phone on arrival and he'll arrange a meeting somewhere private. He'll give you the details on Kitamura's places of accommodation, his movements, private, social, business and political, the people he sees and mixes with, family, friends and others, and his personal interests. In short, you will know as much as you need to know about the man. The way you operate from there will then be entirely up to you. You will not carry a firearm. You will of course be able to contact at least one of us around the clock.'

Steiner turned to Arnall. 'I can leave tomorrow morning if we can sort out the details today. My arrival in Tokyo will then be early on Thursday morning. What about Shimada?'

'Excellent,' said Arnall. 'You'll have everything you need today and I'll contact Shimada. I know he's in Tokyo this week.'

'Does he know about me?' said Steiner.

'We told him yesterday that we have someone in mind and that he'll probably be there this week,' said Easter. 'We'll confirm your time of arrival as soon as we book the seat.'

Arnall addressed the three officers. 'If there's nothing else you can leave and put together the stuff James will need.' The three officers left the room.

'I'm really glad you're going,' said Arnall. 'I don't for a second think it'll be an easy job getting hold of

Kitamura but I believe you can do it. You'll always be able to get hold of me on my mobile and I'll also give you my home number. The money will be paid in full, whether or not you get him, and you'll be given a large sum of cash to take with you. I'll need a photograph for the visa. We can get that taken now. The visa, the airline ticket, the cash and the small package the others are preparing will be sent to you by courier this afternoon. Do you have anything else?'

'No,' said Steiner. 'I assume you'll tell your boss Craig Holden I'm going. I'll feel happier knowing we're not alone. After my meeting with Shimada I'll ring you and tell you my plans. I think my only chance of getting him without risk of interference will be outside Tokyo, possibly at his residence in Oku-Nikko. I'd then have to get him to the airport.'

'Do you know the area?' said Arnall. 'I heard you spent most of your time in Tokyo.'

'I did, said Steiner. 'That's where I trained and had a flat. Nikko is a large nature reserve and very beautiful. I know the main part reasonably well but I've never been to Oku-Nikko. If you don't know, that means Inner Nikko, and it is further inland on the other side of the Konsei Pass. I've only seen photographs of it and it is an isolated, mountainous, and densely forested region, interspersed with rivers, lakes and valleys. Lake Ozenuma is in the centre and Ozegahara, a large marsh, in the west. It is three hours by train from Ueno in Tokyo to Numata, the principal town in the region. Nikko town provides access to the main part of the reserve and houses the magnificent mausolea erected over the tombs of Ieyasu Tokugawa, founder of the Tokugawa *shogunate*, and his grandson Iemitsu. Quite simply, the reserve is the very best nature has given us, dangerous as it can be.'

'I hope you don't have to go there to get him. It

sounds bleak and inhospitable. How would you ever get him out?'

'I'm not there yet,' said Steiner getting to his feet. 'If there's nothing else I'll leave you. Thank you for the job.'

'I'm not sure I like you going,' said Arnall, 'but it is important. Please ring me as soon as you get there. Good luck James.'

Arnall waited until Steiner had gone and returned to her office. Any doubts she had about the operation were dispelled by Steiner now being included. He had that presence. She lifted the phone and rang a Swedish number. It was to Tore Enoksen and he answered.

'Tore, Ruth Arnall; things are starting to move. The guy I wanted flies to Tokyo tomorrow morning.'

'Excellent,' said Enoksen. 'Is he one of yours? You said you might bring in someone else.'

'He is an independent,' said Arnall. 'He did a job in South Africa and an ex-colleague told me about him. I like him and if anyone can do it I think he can. The biggest problem is the lack of real evidence. Everything is circumstantial and would not convict Kitamura even though it points strongly in his direction. For all we know it could have been one of his men.'

'That's not good for us,' said Enoksen. 'In reality you can't bring him back without the evidence. Releasing him on the street without proof or a confession would create an enormous stench, particularly when it would be made known that he was forcibly removed from Japan by an agent. How are you going to deal with such an eventuality?'

'We will make the decision when the time comes,' said Arnall. 'The present plan is to bring him in without anyone knowing, including his lawyers. We would then grill him and, failing to get a DNA match or anything else, release him, denying any involvement in or knowledge of the incident. If we don't take the risk and don't get what we want, Kitamura will go free.'

'You have my support,' said Enoksen. 'I appreciate what you're doing.'

After the call, Arnall sat quietly at her desk. She was putting her career and that of others at risk, and if the plan failed, they'd all be suspended and dismissed, possibly facing charges and prison sentences. She was about to attend to other matters when Craig Holden opened the door and entered.

'What's the latest on the Kitamura case?' said Holden, taking a seat. 'We need an answer from our people so we know where we stand.'

'We've heard from them,' said Arnall. 'It's negative as expected. Even if we had an extradition treaty, we have no hard evidence without a perfect DNA match.'

'Then there's nothing more we can do,' said Holden. 'He'll go free. He's a future prime minister and aside from anything else that makes him virtually untouchable.'

'I'll try again,' said Arnall. Holden had a certain appeal and she could see why women found him attractive.

Chapter 8

Knightsbridge, London SW7

'Thank you,' said Steiner taking the package from the courier. It was from Ruth Arnall. He closed the door of his house and went into the lounge. It was six-thirty in the evening and Kirsty Callard was watching the news.

'I'm glad that's come,' she said when she saw the package. 'Now you can get it out of the way and concentrate on me.'

Steiner opened the package and extracted the contents. 'JAL tickets, Japanese yen and the blurb,' he said. 'At least I'm going to a country I like.'

'I'd like to go with you one day,' said Callard. 'What time is your flight?'

'Nine in the morning,' said Steiner. 'I'll reach Narita Airport at six on Thursday morning and be at the Hyatt Regency Hotel in Shinjuku two hours later.' He walked over to her. 'After I've read this I'll give Weisz a ring and tell him I'm going. I'd also like you to read this. You'll then know as much as I do.'

Steiner spent the next fifteen minutes reading the notes in the package. They told him little more than he'd heard at the briefing and gave him the work address and phone numbers, work, private and mobile, of Kenichi Shimada, his main contact. He passed the notes to Callard. 'I've already told you this but you might come up with something I should know before I go. I'll ring Weisz.' He rang Weisz at home.

'Bruce, James Steiner. I've told Ruth Arnall I'll go to Japan.'

'I thought you would,' said Weisz. 'I don't particularly like it, and you're doing them a favour, whatever they're paying you.'

'It's enough,' said Steiner, 'and will come in useful.

If the job had been anywhere else, I wouldn't have accepted. It's risky enough without going to unknown territory.'

'You wouldn't have taken it if it meant South Africa?' said Weisz. 'I thought you liked it out here.'

'I won't answer that,' said Steiner. 'I hope Rohm, Bale and Conran are still in jail and that life really means life. It doesn't out here.'

'It'll be for life,' said Weisz. 'When the death penalty was abolished the protesters were partly appeased by the assurance that life would be nothing less. When are you going?'

'First thing tomorrow,' said Steiner. 'I'll let you know how I get on. This guy is no lightweight and I wouldn't be surprised if he has links in the Republic.'

'Look after yourself,' said Weisz. 'I might need you again.'

'Thanks,' said Steiner. 'I like it when you say that. It makes me feel wanted.'

Chapter 9

Chelsea, London SW3

'Shingen Kitamura,' said the man. 'I'm a friend phoning from London.' He shifted the mouthpiece slightly and sank into his chair. It was eleven o'clock at night, seven in the morning in Tokyo. Kitamura came to the phone.

'Arnall's got the person she wanted,' said the man. 'He leaves for Tokyo on the nine o'clock JAL flight to Narita. He is booked in at the Hyatt Regency Hotel in Shinjuku.'

'She has moved quickly,' said Kitamura. 'What's his name?'

'James Steiner. He's English and spent time in Tokyo.'

'Is that why he's been selected?' said Kitamura.

'Partly,' said the man. 'He also did two jobs for the Directorate: Special Operations in South Africa. Their success in bringing those involved to trial was largely up to him.'

'Are you talking about the four South African government ministers who were killed?' said Kitamura.

'That was the more recent case. You've heard about it?'

'Who hasn't?' said Kitamura. 'A very close friend of mine was one of those convicted.' He didn't elaborate. 'I can deal with Steiner but I'd still like to be kept up to date from your side. He'll be in regular contact with Arnall. Who is his contact in Tokyo? There must someone?'

'He is *keishi-kan* Kenichi Shimada of the Tokyo MPD,' said the man. 'We think a deputy of his is in on it but we don't have his name. There's no hard evidence against you and they are desperate to get hold

37

of your DNA to match with the blood on the knife. The other stuff is circumstantial.'

'That's what I like to hear,' said Kitamura, 'and even if they had my DNA they wouldn't get a positive match. I didn't kill her. The knife was stolen from my room the day before. I had sex with her and I wanted more, but the bitch walked out and I let her go. My concern is that I don't want a hint of any involvement in such a sordid affair to reach people out here. To some, only the slightest suspicion means you're guilty and it would destroy me politically. I don't like it that your people have the nerve to send someone over here to drag me back.'

'I understand perfectly,' said the man, 'and I'll do what I can to help you.'

'I appreciate that,' said Kitamura. 'Your friend is still with you in this? He's important.'

'Yes, he wouldn't have it any other way, and is highly capable. Arnall's effectively running her own show with three officers. She knows she wouldn't get authorisation and support for the operation. She is motivated by her relationship with the Enoksen family.'

'That can only be to our advantage,' said Kitamura. 'When and if it suits you to expose her, and if I decide to, she will be thrown to the dogs with no one to support her. She'll be seen as an ill-disciplined eccentric with no credibility. Stay in contact.'

Chapter 10

Chelsea, London SW3

'That was fantastic!' Jane Easter cried. She rolled over to look at Mercer. 'We can't go on shagging like this without others finding out.'

'I hope you're not complaining and feeling guilty because you like being screwed,' said Mercer. 'This is the best sex I've had in a relationship, and when you find it, it's worth getting as much as you can. I don't care if others find out, but I'm not going to run round telling them. It's nice having a bit of privacy.'

'No one else has made me climax every time,' said Easter, 'and with such intensity. You really understand a woman's body. I never knew the G-spot existed and where to find it until you came along. I'm quite happy to keep this quiet. I think Ruth already knows.'

'I think she fancies James Steiner,' said Mercer, 'and I don't think she's getting enough from the present guy. Since meeting him she's lost the smile on her face that goes with regular sex. I don't know what she sees in him.'

'What do you think of Steiner's chances of grabbing Kitamura?' said Easter. 'He must have something going for him otherwise Ruth wouldn't have gone for him.'

'His chances are close to zero,' said Mercer. 'No one can walk into Japan, the second biggest economy in the world, and abduct one of their leading politicians. He'll be finished before he makes his first move.'

'You sound very sure,' said Easter. 'I hope you're wrong but let's concentrate on why we're here. I want some more before I go. I'll show you a great position. It's called *splitting the cicada*. It's one of the nine *tantric* sex techniques described in *Positions of the*

Dark Girl from sixth-century China.'

Chapter 11

Knightsbridge, London SW7

'Ring me as soon as you get to the hotel,' said Kirsty. 'I don't like you going away on something like this without me.' It was six o'clock in the morning and Steiner was leaving for Heathrow Airport.

'You'll be the first to hear from me,' said Steiner. 'I've decided to see Chinen *sensei* and tell him what I'm doing. He's been around the block and I'd like to hear what he has to say.'

'Do you think that's smart?' said Kirsty. 'You're supposed to be working alone and the fewer who know about it the better. What will you say if he tries to dissuade you from going ahead?'

'I won't stop what I've started,' said Steiner. 'I've given Ruth my word and won't let her down. If she decides against it I'll back off. I believe Kitamura is guilty and want to see him face trial.' He kissed her. 'Take care of yourself.'

Chapter 12

Knightsbridge, London SW7

Kirsty Callard didn't like Steiner going off alone on a job even though he knew the country. Kitamura was an extremely powerful, respected politician who would have strong allies and friends, and she didn't need reminding how difficult and hazardous it had been to nail Andrew Rohm. The plan to isolate Kitamura and get him onto a plane was ambitious, even for those with a vivid imagination of what could be achieved when the chances were stacked heavily against them.

An hour after Steiner had left for Heathrow, Callard phoned Ruth Arnall at work.

'Ruth, Kirsty Callard, Steiner's girlfriend.'

'He told me about you,' said Arnall. 'I hope things are alright and he's on his way.'

'He left an hour ago,' said Callard, 'but I wanted to speak to you. I'm worried about this job. What are his chances of pulling it off? This is not his game.'

'It is as much his game as anyone else's,' said Arnall. 'I did not go for James lightly. I only had to meet him and remember what was said about him to know I'd made the right choice. This is a tough job and we're asking a lot but if there is any sign of danger we'll bring him back.'

'You won't know and it might be too late,' said Callard.

'That's a risk,' said Arnall, 'but one that we have to take. The only consolation I can give besides my confidence in James is that he'll be bringing in someone who brutally murdered an innocent girl. As far as we could see she'd been stabbed seven times in the chest and abdomen.'

'I have confidence in James,' said Kirsty. 'I've seen

him in action. I wanted to hear it from you.'

'I understand,' said Arnall. 'Please ring me again if you want to but I've a suspicion you'll be the first to know what happens out there.'

'Perhaps,' said Callard, 'but not when he's in trouble.'

Chapter 13

Shinjuku, Tokyo

Steiner landed at Narita International Airport at six, and, after clearing immigration, caught the limousine bus to Shinjuku in Tokyo and the Hyatt Regency Hotel. He had a two-room suite on the seventh floor with a magnificent view of Mt Fuji. After a shower, he phoned Kenichi Shimada at his office. He answered.

'Shimada *san*, James Steiner. Good morning. I'm at my hotel.'

'James *san*, welcome to Japan,' said Shimada. 'I hope you had a pleasant flight.'

'Very nice thank you,' said Steiner. 'Where would you like to meet?'

'I can be at the hotel in thirty minutes,' said Shimada. 'Give me your room number and we'll meet there.'

'773,' said Steiner. 'I look forward to it.' He cut the call. Shimada didn't want to be seen with him. Arnall was right. He'd be working alone.

Thirty minutes later, Shimada knocked on the door and Steiner let him in. The suite was designed for business meetings and they sat at a round table in the second room.

'I believe Commander Arnall has told you everything she knows,' said Shimada, 'and you understand I'm here to provide you with whatever details I have of Kitamura's movements. I can't offer you direct support but I will help make arrangements if necessary when you're ready to leave with Kitamura. I didn't tell Arnall but they've probably guessed that my boss, superintendent general of the Tokyo MPD, *keishi-sokan*, knows what's going on. I won't go into details but he assigned me the job of helping you because he wants Kitamura brought down. A deputy of mine is in on it but nobody knows who. It has to be like that. He is Chief Superintendent, *keishi-cho*, Kokichi Maruyama. It stops with those two. I'm confident the superintendent general's boss, the commissioner general of the National Police Agency, is in the dark but he was the first in the police to know about the request from the British and instructed the superintendent general not to pursue it. Japanese politics comprises powerful factions, and it's not always easy to know who you can trust. A leak in the wrong place about something others don't like could mean your immediate elimination. The same principle applies to all important relationships in life does it not?'

'I won't disagree on that,' said Steiner, 'and thank you for being open. I feel better.'

'It's still daylight,' said Shimada, smiling briefly. 'No, we think you are safe. You can trust me and Maruyama, and my boss has seen a few things. He can smell his enemies and despises Kitamura. I'm not saying there are not others who knew of your people's request and vehemently opposed it but they think the issue is dead and don't know anything about this plan.'

'I hope you are right,' said Steiner, 'otherwise I should catch the next flight home. Why do you and the others support the plan?'

'We have no evidence, and it is unknown to the vast majority, but Kitamura was heavily involved with the *yakuza*,' said Shimada. 'He became extremely powerful and established his own clan, independent of traditional ties. It is shrouded in secrecy and part of its strength is that very few members or associates know Kitamura is the head, like the Casalesi clan of the Camorra, the Neapolitan mafia. For this reason we want to see Kitamura put away for life. We don't care where it is, and the evidence you have is the best we've seen. You might know that the main activities of the *yakuza* are amphetamines, or *shabu*, prostitution, gambling, protection, racketeering and people trafficking from Asia to Europe. Cocaine hardly figures in their operations – because of exchange deals with the police by which limited distribution of amphetamines is ignored – but Kitamura has developed very strong links with Colombian cartels and we don't want the drug to gain a base in Japan, as it has in Europe, Africa and the USA. At present most of his attention has been on Europe and Africa but unless we are very careful that will change. Amphetamines is the most widely used illegal drug in Japan and the fourth most widely used drug after caffeine, alcohol and nicotine. Older people attach a lot of shame to its use because it was freely given to Japan's armed forces during WWII, the lost war.'

'How do you know about Kitamura's activities without having any evidence?' said Steiner.

'Through a well-established network of informers,' said Shimada, 'that only a group like ours can create. The problem frequently found with informers is that they can "see" but are rarely in a position to "get". Therefore we lack hard evidence, and without it, everything is mere speculation. When someone becomes wealthy there are always rumours about how it is achieved, but successful criminals rapidly acquire immunity to rumours and carry on regardless, meticulously covering their tracks.'

'Tell me about Kitamura's movements,' said Steiner.

'He spends most weekends at his place just outside the western border of Oku-Nikko,' said Shimada. 'He also has an apartment in Chiyoda and is there during the week. Chiyoda is one of the wards of Tokyo and contains the Imperial Palace, the Diet and the prime minister's residence. Kantei, the office of the prime minister, is in Nagatacho, a neighbourhood of Chiyoda. It's a beautiful area.'

'Chiyoda isn't good for me,' said Steiner. 'I've been there before. It has a perfect, manicured landscape and is too quiet. I'd stand out. There are also national guards patrolling the area at night.'

'I agree,' said Shimada, 'and that leaves his place in Oku-Nikko. Its remote location gives it the advantage over Tokyo but that's where it ends. Since returning from London, and perhaps because he's aware of his guilt, Kitamura has two or more bodyguards constantly at his side. Some politicians use bodyguards, but Kitamura never did until now.'

'Surely that's not a coincidence,' said Steiner. 'Do you know or recognise these people?' He looked at Shimada closely. 'Gary Mercer, an officer of Arnall's and involved in this case, said Kitamura runs a clandestine martial arts school. Arnall dismissed it as fiction. Clive Dance, another officer, said reference to the school came from you.'

'The two officers and another, a woman officer, were present when I spoke to Arnall on the phone,' said Shimada. 'That was when I made the comment. Arnall dismissed it then but it is true. Three of the men seen here in Tokyo with Kitamura are involved with his school.'

'Do you have their names?' said Steiner.

'Two are British, David Tate and Carl Norman, and the third is Japanese, Shuji Oda,' said Shimada. 'They are clever, arrogant and merciless. Why do you ask?'

'They were with Kitamura at his hotel in London,' said Steiner. 'Do you think they could have killed the girl on behalf of Kitamura? It's not exactly unusual for a guy's henchmen to do his dirty work or what he should do himself. The blood on the knife could belong to one of them.'

'That has to be possible,' said Shimada. 'If you manage to get Kitamura back to London and the DNA doesn't match, you might have to return for those guys.'

'I didn't hear that,' said Steiner, 'and I have a request. I'd like you to get the DNA profile of the blood on the knife sent to you. Perhaps the Met is too sure that it belongs to Kitamura and are jumping ahead, concentrating only on his physical return and conviction. I appreciate that London would like the body present so they can take the sample and avoid a dispute concerning its source but I'm talking about elimination and finding the real killer. If we have the DNA sample and can get one here from Kitamura, we might find they don't match and will have to think again.'

Shimada nodded. 'I'll have the DNA profile sent over.'

'Thank you,' said Steiner. 'Now back to Kitamura's movements.'

'First, let me tell you a bit more about Tate, Norman and Oda and the martial arts school that Arnall regards as a figment of my imagination,' said Shimada. 'You've heard of MMA, or mixed martial arts? Tate is a born killer in the ring, unbeaten, and he, Norman and Oda are champions. They're in the top five in Asia and have already beaten the leading Europeans and Americans.'

'I've heard of it,' said Steiner, 'and who hasn't? It's a combat sport played out with rules in a cage or ring. The major governing body is UFC or Ultimate Fighting Championship from the USA and it is sometimes called cage fighting.'

'Exactly,' said Shimada. 'I suspect that with your training it's not your game. Am I right?'

'Yes,' said Steiner. 'Cage fighting or beating someone to a pulp in a ring does not suit my mentality. The reasoning behind MMA is that the best fighter or ultimate fighter is one who is trained in all combat techniques. Unlike arts like *karate*, *judo*, boxing and wrestling which concentrate on striking or grappling, any technique is used in training and these are recognised and permissible in contests. MMA is not a new concept. It goes back centuries and the premise that this approach makes the best fighter is crap. The best fighter is the one with the mental strength who can adapt to the situation and prevailing circumstances, like life, and is not the person who has practised the most techniques. In my school of *karate*, and the leading *aikido* school, we practise techniques with the single aim of developing mental strength and the power that derives from mind and body coordination. There are hundreds of possible techniques but the aim is that only one should be necessary in any situation. There is variety so that beginners don't get bored, but in reality, practising only a few techniques until they are perfect is the name of the game. That is how the old masters trained. I'm not saying that a person who has trained in MMA hasn't developed considerable mental power. Some of them are very powerful and formidable fighters, and would be a match for highly ranked people who have followed the traditional path. Are you going to tell me that Kitamura's school is for MMA?'

'No,' said Shimada. 'It goes far deeper than that, back to the root of Japan's martial disciplines. I'm sure you know much of what I'm going to tell you but it is worth emphasising because it will give you a better understanding of who we're up against in Kitamura, where he has deviated and what makes him and his people so dangerous.'

'I'm listening,' said Steiner. 'I get the feeling I'm

going to learn something.'

'The Japanese arts such as *karatedo*, *aikido*, *judo* and *kendo* are modern martial arts, or modern *budo*,' said Shimada, 'and were systemised after 1868, the end of the feudal period. The true classical warrior of Japan is the professional fighting man who rose to political power with the inauguration of Japan's first *shogun*, Minamoto Yoritomo, and the inception of the Kamakura military government, *bakufu*, in 1185. This breed of warrior was known as *bushi* and the term also described the professional warriors of similar type, position and status who prevailed throughout the feudal era, at times with markedly less influence. The importance of the Kamakura *bushi* is that they were in a class apart, ethically, morally and in fighting ability from the conscript soldiers and *bushi* of later years and were the driving force behind the development of the classical martial arts or *bujutsu*. The code of conduct, *bushido*, adopted and esteemed by the *bushi* was of loyalty, honour and courage and the foundation of these virtues was rigid discipline, frugality and a devotion to the growth of the martial arts. For four centuries, martial culture in the form of *bujutsu* was pre-eminent in Japan's history and the details of 9 000 styles or *ryu* were transcribed on scrolls, *makimono*, for future generations. The inception of the first Tokugawa *shogunate* in 1603 took Japan into a relatively peaceful period and the portrait of the classical *bushi* as an elite group of warriors with the intrinsic virtues of courage, sound judgement and courtesy became through enforced government edicts a symbol of the past.'

'Are you going to tell me Kitamura sees himself as a modern *bushi*?' said Steiner.

'I'm coming to that,' said Shimada laconically. 'A significant aspect of the Tokugawa feudal period was that it spawned the classical Japanese *budo*, those disciplines, like the modern *budo* I mentioned earlier, that had spiritual development rather than combat proficiency as their aim and which drew extensively in their physical dimension on the combat techniques of *bujutsu*. The major reason for the birth of *budo* was that in the immediate pre-Tokugawa period thousands upon thousands of *bushi* were killed in battles between rival feudal lords, the *daimyo*. Consequently, in the early Tokugawa period, the *bushi*, spiritually depleted and controlled by government directives, turned to the development of spiritual disciplines in a general desire for peaceful existence between men. The *bujutsu* – designed as efficient methods of hand-to-hand combat for the *bushi* or aristocratic few – no longer served the *bakufu*. Military policy was for the use of firearms and the deployment of large numbers of conscript soldiers. The *bushi*, as members of military families, the *buke*, and in accordance with this change in emphasis, maintained their status on a hereditary basis rather than through exemplary military service, and were expected to participate in non-martial pursuits such as the tea ceremony. The *do* concept as in *budo* was to the Japanese not a religion but a way to follow in life, a way beset by technical and physical hardship which had to be overcome for personal development and the attainment of self-perfection, *satori*. Practitioners of *budo* came to appreciate that emphasis on technical form ensured self-discipline which in turn nurtured and served the spirit. After years of training, form was dispensed with and self-perfection achieved, or artless art. The *do* forms were intrinsically linked to the *zen* method which had *satori* and ultimately enlightenment, *nirvana*, as its goal. Like *zen*, the *do* methods of spiritual development were simple and direct, qualities which appealed to the *bushi*. The *zen* method had served the *bushi* in pre-Tokugawa times and it was well understood that the quality of technical performance depended on the mind of the performer and that spiritual power was the essence of mastery.'

Steiner listened patiently. Shimada knew he would be well versed in the development of the *bushi* arts and the systematic development of *budo*, but relating it was his way of getting to what Steiner knew was coming. He had heard it before, justification for living on the dark side of life.

'The Tokugawa era ended in 1868,' said Shimada, 'and the feudal period of Japanese history was over. The new government was controlled by men of *samurai* rank. The term *samurai*, though frequently misused today to mean the ultimate classical warrior by Hollywood film directors, denotes 'service', and correctly translated means 'one who serves'. In the early feudal period it did not specifically refer to the classical warrior. In the fifteenth century the term was used to describe a category of *bushi*, but by no means the highest. In the Tokugawa or Edo period there were different ranks within the *samurai* class itself, but after 1868 the term *samurai* was extended to become synonymous with *bushi*, the professional warriors of the time, those allowed to wear the *daisho*, the long and short swords. As a class of fighting men the *samurai* or *bushi* of the Tokugawa era were not of the same high calibre as the *bushi* of the pre-Tokugawa period mentally, physically and spiritually, and in terms of the extraordinary internal power derived from the conditioning of the unconscious mind, the *zen* mind.'

Shimada drank some coffee and stared at Steiner. 'You are one of the few who has drawn on the original teachings of the *bushi* through your training in one of the best schools of modern *budo*, specifically *karatedo*, and have become very powerful. I am sure the ethics and code of conduct at the centre of these arts have been ingrained in you, but that is not always the case with others who have undergone such training. Selective interpretation of noble beliefs and philosophies has often been made by people to justify a base need for serious criminal activity that already exists within them. Darwin's theory of evolution by natural selection, survival of the fittest, was used to justify the creation of a master race by the Nazis because they claimed they were assisting nature. Perverse interpretation of sections of religious text has been used to justify persecution of people of other faiths. The Nationalists in South Africa, devout Calvinists, satisfied their dislike of the blacks and their desire for apartheid by restrictively and literally interpreting parts of the Bible to suit. Muslim fundamentalists have done the same thing with the Koran as they exhort terrorism and murder against western society to eliminate perceived immorality. Many would take what I've told you about the *bushi* and the code of *bushido* to enhance the way they live their lives, but Kitamura is not one of them. The artefacts in the museum on his estate reflects his obsession with the early Japanese feudal period, but the methods taught in his training school centres on the physical techniques and methods devised by the *bushi*, for use in war, to destroy human life whenever it stands in the way of his criminal activities. Kitamura distorts the principles to justify extreme violence when torturing and killing those who oppose him. He sees himself not as a *bushi*, but as a *daimyo*, the feudal lord who employed the *bushi*. The school provides a progressive step for those already steeped in the brutality perpetrated in MMA and cage fighting, or those who have an innate thirst for violence.'

'Why doesn't he do what the mafia does and hire men with guns to wipe out the opposition?' said

Steiner. 'It's very efficient and they seldom make mistakes. With them it's down to a fine art.'

'It's his brand of perversion,' said Shimada. 'He's a psychopath who likes feudal methods because they lend themselves to cruelty and torture. His people use guns when it suits them, but the techniques prohibited in the ring are their preference and more satisfying than killing someone cleanly.'

'Charming,' said Steiner. 'I've seen it before, sometimes displayed by people on the mat, but not as you describe it. You are telling me that Kitamura, a future prime minister, uses methods of extreme and unnecessary violence to control a criminal empire of which the police have no evidence.'

'Yes,' said Shimada, 'but I tell you only as a warning. You are going into an extremely hostile, merciless world when you go against Kitamura and set foot on that estate.'

'What about Kitamura's movements?' said Steiner.

'He leaves late afternoon on Fridays for Oku-Nikko and returns on Monday morning. You came at the right time because this Friday he is going there for a week before the next session of the Diet. There are two main routes to Nikko from Tokyo, one to Nikko town on the east side of the reserve, and the other through Numata city to Kamata. Numata is the gateway to Oku-Nikko, lies on a plateau overlooking the Katashina, Usune and Tone rivers, and is an ancient Edo-period merchant centre. At Kamata the road branches and goes north-east to Lake Sugenuma, just inside the reserve, and north to Oshimizu, three hours by bus from Numata. You want Oshimizu and from there to Lake Ozenuma, eight kilometres north by road. The scenery is unbelievably beautiful.'

'I hope we're getting close,' said Steiner phlegmatically. 'Where does Kitamura hang out?'

'Lake Ozenuma is surrounded by mountains,' said Shimada. 'Seven kilometres going west by road is Ozegahara, a large marsh. Kitamura's estate is two kilometres from the marsh.'

'It's in the middle of nowhere,' said Steiner, 'and I'm supposed to pull him out.'

'Yes,' said Shimada, 'unless you choose Chiyoda. But do not despair. Later this morning I'll receive a detailed map of the estate and the surrounding area. I arranged for it to be prepared because I thought you would decide to go there.'

'You think of everything,' said Steiner. 'Who's getting it for you? I thought only you and Maruyama are involved.'

'The man lives in Tokyo and used to work on the estate as a servant,' said Shimada. 'It is perfectly safe and he has never had any direct contact with Kitamura. The map will be very useful to you.'

'What other information have you got besides the map?' said Steiner. 'Where and when does Kitamura eat, sleep and bath? Does he have any particular habits? Does he walk around his estate regularly at a specific time? Does he venture off the estate when he goes there? Who are his servants on the estate and are they close? Does he have a family or other relatives who live or travel with him? Does he have close friends in the area who he visits? Is there a secretary or personal assistant with him? Where is the training school located? Do the men who train there live on the estate and are they locals or, like the two British, from abroad? The more I have the easier it will be. I want to build a picture so I won't waste time trying to work things out when I get there. I want as few surprises as possible. I assume there won't be anyone I can speak to when I get there.'

'You'll be totally on your own,' said Shimada. 'The

map won't be the only thing you get. Maruyama is working on the other stuff and we'll give you what we've got when we meet again. There's also a small *ryokan* we know of two kilometres from the estate. You might need a place for rest, depending on the time.'

'When will we meet again?' said Steiner. 'I'd like to know when and how Kitamura leaves for the estate and who'll be with him. If you can't be precise, the fact he's going late tomorrow will be enough.'

'Maruyama and I will meet you here in your room at eight tomorrow morning,' said Shimada. 'From what you've heard, how do you intend to move?'

'I'd like a car,' said Steiner, 'a used four-door saloon, nothing new. A Lexus will do. I'd also like a pair of Nikon binoculars, 12x36. They might help to see what's going on without being too close. I've got the other things I might need.'

'Welcome to the real world James *san*,' said Shimada. 'But you've been there before.'

'I'm not used to this sort of thing,' said Steiner. 'If there is anything else, please tell me.'

'There is something that might come in very useful, and which I shouldn't be offering to you,' said Shimada.

'What is it?' said Steiner. 'I want to keep things simple.'

A firearm,' said Shimada. 'Like your people, we don't carry them, and they are only used by special operatives in specific situations. But I think you need one, going alone on a job like this. It's a semi-automatic pistol with a silencer and laser flashlight. The model is a silenced Beretta *90two* 9mmx19 Luger/Parabellum with a Burris light.'

Steiner looked at him for a while then said: 'I declined such an offer before, but I accept. There are too many out there who've got guns and know how to use them. I've had a couple of close calls which could have gone either way. What do I do with it if we don't meet again?'

'Wipe it clean and dump it,' said Shimada. 'It can't be traced. It takes 17 rounds and will be full. You'll also get a spare clip. I don't think you'll need any more.'

Steiner got up and held out his hand. 'I appreciate what you're doing. We'll meet tomorrow.' Shimada shook his hand and left the room.

Chapter 14

The Japanese Prime Minister's Residence
Nagatacho, Chiyoda, Tokyo

'I don't want to go back to London when I'm innocent,' said Kitamura. 'It would look as if I was involved and a prime suspect. Some might even conclude I'm guilty and it would destroy me politically.' The Japanese prime minister was seated across the desk from him.

'To others it would show you have nothing to hide and fear,' said the prime minister, 'but I understand your reasoning. I believe what you have told me and to me that's what counts. If it was ever proved you were guilty of such a terrible crime, I would also be vilified and the family name disgraced. I have instructed the commissioner general of the NPA not to act on the case. As a Japanese national you would never be extradited. Let's leave it at that.'

'Yes,' said Kitamura, rising and giving a bow. 'Thank you for your trust in me. I would never betray you.'

Chapter 15

Grosvenor House Hotel, London W1

'As much as I love South Africa it's good to be here,' said Andrew Rohm. It was ten o'clock in the morning and he was sitting with his English lawyer, Peter Levy, in the lounge of the Grosvenor House Hotel on Park Lane. Three hours earlier, he had been met by a driver at Heathrow Airport.

'Especially after prison,' said Levy. 'I had a feeling it wouldn't take you long to get out. What are your plans? I've already got five houses for you to look at.' He took some agents' property lists from his case and placed them in front of Rohm. 'They're in Belgravia.'

'Excellent,' said Rohm. 'I want to see some of my business associates. They're in London and I'm keen to step up activity in some areas. Africa is a massive market and my operations can be controlled as easily from here as in the Republic.'

'I was coming to that,' said Levy. 'Shingen Kitamura is wanted for questioning by Scotland Yard for the murder of a Swedish girl in Hyde Park.'

Rohm lifted his eyes from the papers and stared at him. 'Kitamura killed a girl in London? Is this some kind of joke?'

'No,' said Levy. 'I wouldn't joke about something like that. She was a student Kitamura picked up at the Whisky Mist club in the Hilton Hotel. He took her back to the Dorchester where he was staying. It appears she left an hour later and was found stabbed to death by a park attendant early on Sunday morning. When she left, Kitamura followed. He returned a short time later.'

'Is that all the evidence the police have got?' said Rohm. 'Did anyone see him follow her into Hyde Park?'

'Apparently not,' said Levy. 'A knife was found in a bin with her blood and that from someone else on it. The knife is very unusual and a Japanese man of Kitamura's age bought a similar one from a shop in Burlington Arcade a couple of days previously. I don't know any more except it's logical to assume the police want to see if the DNA on the knife matches Kitamura's. They don't have his and can't get him back here because he's a national and there's no extradition treaty between the UK and Japan. It's been in the press but has dried up.'

'And that's where it stands?' said Rohm. 'I must give him a ring. He has begun to play a very important part in my operations. He has contacts in the Far East and that's an area where we see considerable expansion, not only in cocaine and heroin, but in animal products. He has homes in Tokyo and Oku-Nikko.'

'Do you still own a place in Japan?' said Levy. 'You went there several times from South Africa.'

'Yes,' said Rohm. 'I've got a flat in Ginza. It's Tokyo's Belgravia.' He glanced at the property lists. 'I'm going to give Kitamura a ring and then we'll go and see these. Perhaps you can fix up some times with the agents.'

'I'll do that now,' said Levy.

Rohm left the reception and went up to his room. He checked his address book and dialled Kitamura's Tokyo number. He answered.

'Shingen, Andrew Rohm. I'm in London. How are you?'

'Andrew,' said Kitamura. 'You were in jail in South Africa.'

'I'm here now,' said Rohm. 'I got out and arrived here this morning. I'll tell you more another time. I hear you're in a bit of trouble.'

'Yes,' said Kitamura. 'The British think I killed a Swedish girl in Hyde Park and want me to return for questioning.'

'Why not, if you're innocent?' said Rohm.

'I am innocent and it might look good to some by returning voluntary,' said Kitamura, 'but others might think I've been forced to return because I'm guilty. I don't want that conveyed to the Japanese public, and prefer to proclaim my innocence from here. If I returned the British would try to pin whatever they can on me to show they've caught the killer.'

'What about the knife you bought and the blood stain?' said Rohm.

'That's what I mean,' said Kitamura. 'The knife was stolen from my hotel room the day before and they have no proof the blood is mine. They're trying anything to get their hands on me.'

'But they're unable to,' said Rohm, 'and in your position I'd be inclined to do as you're doing. You've made your decision, and without any hard evidence to sway public opinion against you, the issue will go away. I'd like to come and see you. There's a lot to discuss.'

'There is,' said Kitamura, 'but there's something else. Ruth Arnall the commander in the Met's Specialist Crime Directorate, has sent someone to Japan to take me back to the UK.'

'Don't tell me she's acting without authorisation,' said Rohm.

'She is,' said Kitamura, 'unless she's confiding in someone we don't know about. I've nothing to substantiate an accusation against them without drawing attention to a friend. I decided to let them come to me. The man they've chosen is already in Tokyo. You might have heard of him. He previously worked for South Africa's Directorate: Special

Operations and was a member of the team that put you behind bars.'

'Then I have heard of him,' said Rohm, 'but I can't think of anyone working for them who would now be with the Met. There are plenty in the UK who are queuing up to get in. Do you have his name?'

'James Steiner,' said Kitamura. 'He was an independent operator for the Scorpions and is English. He lives in central London.'

'I certainly know him,' said Rohm, his hatred palpable. 'He single-handedly destroyed a lot of what I'd taken years to establish. If there's one person I'd like to put a stake through, it's him. What are you doing about it?'

'I've two choices,' said Kitamura. 'I can see what moves he makes and then nullify him, or deter him before he gets going. He'll never get what he came for. But that's my problem. As soon I've finished with him, come over.'

'I'll do that,' said Rohm. 'I'm looking for a house in London, but you can get me on this number or my mobile. Good luck.' He replaced the receiver, thinking only of Steiner. Another opportunity to remove Steiner might present itself, and if it did, and he could get involved, there'd not be another mistake.

Chapter 16

Shinjuku, Tokyo

'Are you missing me?' said Steiner. 'I'm in my room at the Hyatt Regency Hotel.'

'You know the answer,' said Callard. 'Did you have a nice flight?'

'Yes,' said Steiner. 'I've met Shimada. He'll give me the help his brief allows. We discussed Kitamura's movements and I think it's too risky to try for him in Tokyo.'

'That means Oku-Nikko,' said Kirsty, 'but it's so isolated.'

'I can deal with that as long as I plan carefully,' said Steiner. 'There are things I'd like answers to before I go. Shimada and his sidekick Maruyama are getting them for me and we're meeting in my room tomorrow morning.'

'When will Kitamura be there?' said Kirsty. 'How will you get to the place?'

'He goes there every weekend, but tomorrow it's for a week before the next Diet session,' said Steiner. 'Shimada's getting a car for me and I'll drive there from Tokyo. If there are no problems I could have this wrapped up in a couple of days and be on the plane home.'

'I do hope so,' said Kirsty. 'I spoke to Ruth Arnall and she has every confidence in you.'

'That's nice to hear,' said Steiner. 'I'll try to phone you when I get closer. The nearest town to Kitamura is Numata, and from there it's nothing except lakes, valleys and a large marsh.'

'What a romantic setting,' said Kirsty. 'What are you doing this afternoon?'

'If Morio Chinen is available I'll go and see him,'

said Steiner. 'The *dojo*'s not far from here.'

'Will you tell him why you're there?' said Kirsty.

'Yes,' said Steiner. 'I'd like to hear what he thinks but whatever it is, it won't stop me going ahead. I won't back off on Arnall.'

'It'll be interesting to hear what he says about it,' said Kirsty.

'It will be,' said Steiner. 'Take care of yourself.'

After the call Steiner rang the *karate dojo* in Yoyogi. He'd spent a lot of time training there under the renowned master Morio Chinen. Michiko, the school secretary, answered and Steiner arranged to see the teacher.

Steiner left the hotel and walked to the *dojo*. Thirty minutes later he was drinking tea with Chinen in his office. He explained the reason for his visit to Japan and relayed what Shimada had told him about Kitamura.

'I would have done what you're doing,' said Chinen, 'but you have to be very cautious. Kitamura is not only a popular, successful politician but also a man with extensive business interests in large companies. If the police think he has *yakuza* links and is running his own clan, he is not only formidable, but very dangerous. If on top of that, and as described by Shimada, he sees himself as a modern *daimyo* served by men whose brutal, murderous activities are those of the *bushi* – preferring to forget the honourable code *bushido* to which the *bushi* aspired – then he is, in his deluded state, even more dangerous. Is there any chance Kitamura knows you are here in Tokyo and after him?'

'I don't know the answer,' said Steiner. 'In London, and to my knowledge, only Arnall, her boss and the three officers know I'm here. In Japan, it is only Shimada, his boss and Maruyama. If Kitamura knows

I'm here it can only come from them, but there is no way of knowing unless they reveal themselves. I can only be vigilant.'

'And be aware that there might be a leak,' said Chinen. 'You must not trust anyone more than you have to. Of those people and from what you've told me, I'd only trust Ruth Arnall.'

'Before my experience in South Africa I'd have thought that was being too cautious,' said Steiner, 'but now I agree with you.'

Chinen studied him. 'If there is anyone who can succeed in this, it is you. Your dedicated training in the *do* and the level you have achieved will not desert you. But if there is any help I or the others can give you, tell me.'

'Thank you,' said Steiner. 'There is one thing. After I pick up Kitamura I want to check his DNA with a sample being sent over from London to see if there is a match. I might need someone to help me while the comparison is made, either by watching over Kitamura or by delivering the sample to Shimada.'

'An *uchideshi* will help you,' said Chinen.

'Thank you.' Steiner bowed and left the *dojo*.

Steiner spent the rest of the day in the Shinjuku Central Park, site of the Kumano Shrine and near the hotel. He returned to his room in the late evening, and, after a meal, went to bed.

Chapter 17

Grosvenor House Hotel, London W1

'I like the house in Eaton Place,' said Rohm. 'It's not as prestigious as Eaton Square, but quieter, and the location is perfect. At fifteen million pounds I think it's reasonable. Two years ago a place in this street would have fetched twenty million, but they're going up and will soon pass that figure. You can never beat property in the right location as an investment.'

'I think it's a very good buy,' said Peter Levy, 'and as you say it's on the up as we speak. I can have the place in your hands today. With the furnishings included in the price you can move in tomorrow morning.'

'That suits me,' said Rohm. 'Please arrange it. There's something else I'd like you to do for me. When I spoke to Kitamura he said Arnall had hired someone to go to Japan and bring him back here. Arnall believes he is guilty and is apparently prepared to take the risk that he's not. The person is James Steiner and he was working for the DSO in South Africa when I was a free man. Steiner was the direct cause of my conviction and lives in West London. I want his address for the record. I've a feeling it will come in useful. Kitamura told me he has already arrived in Tokyo.'

'What did Kitamura say he's doing about it?' said Levy.

'Only that he'll deal with him,' said Rohm. 'I think Kitamura will rough him up as a warning and tell him to get out. I don't think he'll kill him. It's risky and could attract attention, but I'm sure that will come later if Steiner refuses to back off and goes for him.'

'And if Steiner does return?' said Levy. 'It sounds as if you'd go after him.'

'I'll consider that if it arises,' said Rohm. 'As much as I want him dead, hatred must not make me careless. I don't like prison, here or in South Africa.'

'What are you going to do now?' said Levy. 'It is early afternoon, the sun is shining and the shops are open until late.'

'I think I'll go for a walk through the park to Knightsbridge and then come back here past my new acquisition in Belgravia,' said Rohm. 'I'll also visit Harrods.'

'Yes, the best department store you can find,' said Levy, 'and even more grandiose since Fayed bought it. I'll phone you in the morning.' He got up and left the hotel.

Chapter 18

Knightsbridge, London SW7

Kirsty was already missing Steiner and after lunch she left the house for a walk. She decided to go down past the Victoria and Albert Museum, up the Brompton Road and back to the house. It was not a long walk, but she had some paper work to complete.

When Kirsty reached the corner with Montpelier Street she stopped. On the other side of the street, and about to head towards Hyde Park, was Andrew Rohm. For a moment he looked at her then continued on his way, as if he had not a care in the world. It was Rohm, of that she was sure, and she had difficulty believing she had just seen a man in London's West End who was supposed to be doing a life sentence in a high-security South African jail. When Callard reached the house she immediately phoned Bruce Weisz.

'Bruce, Kirsty Callard. I'm at the house. I've just seen Andrew Rohm in the street.'

Weisz was quiet then said: 'He escaped from Pollsmoor Prison near Cape Town two days ago, and it's a distinct possibility he left the country.'

'How did he make it?' said Kirsty. 'It's not everyday a guy gets out of there and manages to leave.'

'He was being taken to court for other crimes when the car he was in disappeared,' said Weisz. 'There was no violence or any form of a hit and the break appears to have been well orchestrated. The car and two drivers haven't been found. When the car didn't appear at the court the borders and airlines were checked. There was no Rohm and he had probably changed his identity.'

'Do you think he saw me?' said Kirsty.

'If he did and wants to keep you quiet, he will come after you,' said Weisz. 'I'll contact Ruth Arnall and get someone to watch the house. I'll also see what can be done to find Rohm.'

'I don't want anyone outside the house,' said Callard. 'I'll face him if I have to.'

'It might not take long to find him,' said Weisz. 'He is British, and if he's changed his identity it's likely he'll be on a new British passport. Are you going to phone Steiner?'

'He's got enough to think about,' said Kirsty, 'and he can't do anything over there. Even if he was here he couldn't do anything. It's a problem for the police. They have the experience and resources.'

Chapter 19

Grosvenor House Hotel, Park Lane, London W1

'I have no doubt it was her,' said Rohm. He was speaking to Peter Levy on the phone. 'I'd recognise her anywhere and I'm sure she saw me before outside Harrods. I now regret not getting rid of her then.'

'It's a strange world,' said Levy. 'Steiner's after your friend Kitamura in Japan and you see his lover in London. What are you going to do about it? You realise that if she recognised you she is a major threat. She'll find out you've escaped and fled South Africa, and the DSO with Interpol will be in hot pursuit.'

'I'm aware of that,' said Rohm, 'and for that reason I've got to move quickly to try to eliminate any possible threat. Do you have Steiner's address? It has to be near Harrods.'

'It is,' said Levy, '32 Ennismore Garden Mews. You're close to being neighbours.'

'I want someone I can trust to pick her up,' said Rohm. 'I don't care where they take her as long as she's out of circulation. I'll decide later what to do with her.'

'You realise that by doing that you'll remove any doubt in her mind that she saw you,' said Levy. 'At the moment, she might only think she saw you. You will then have no choice other than to eliminate her permanently.'

'She couldn't have failed to recognise me,' said Rohm. 'She was looking at me when I was on the corner of Montpelier Street on the way to Hyde Park. The risk of exposure is too great for me to ignore. Who do you know? There are people in South Africa who could do it, but I can't wait.'

'I've got just the man,' said Levy, 'but this would be

small stuff for him. I don't think he'd take it.'

'If the price is right he'll do it,' said Rohm confidently. 'Who is he?'

'Phillip Moran,' said Levy. 'Do you know the name?'

'No,' said Rohm. 'You've been keeping quiet about him.'

'He's a professional killer, very selective and untarnished,' said Levy, 'but for the right money I think he'd pick her up and put her away. You don't want an amateur.'

'I'd like him to do it tonight,' said Rohm. 'He'll be paid accordingly. You have the address, and she's attractive enough not to be mistaken for someone else. She's about five-nine, thirty-five with long dark hair. I hope Moran can do the job without lust screwing things up.'

Chapter 20

Mount Street, Mayfair, London W1

When he reached his office, Levy phoned Phillip Moran. He answered.

'Phillip, Peter Levy. I've a small job for you. It's not exactly your line but the money's very good. I'd like it done tonight.'

'I'm very busy,' said Moran, 'but tell me.'

'I want a woman picked up and taken to a house in South Kensington,' said Levy. 'She might resist but you can handle it. You'll have to make sure she stays quiet for a few days until my client decides what to do with her.'

'You're right, it's not my line,' said Moran, 'but if the money's good I'll do it.'

'Twenty-five grand,' said Levy, 'paid into an account of your choice.'

'Your client must want this done badly,' said Moran. 'Where is she? Is she alone? I don't want to have to sort out a lover first.'

'She's alone in a mews house behind the Brompton Oratory in Knightsbridge,' said Levy. 'Her lover's in Japan. There's a chance she recognised my client outside Harrods and he can't take the risk. I'll leave the address for the mews, and the keys and address for the South Kensington house at the front desk of my office. I'm still in Mount Street. The woman is Kirsty Callard, pretty, in her thirties, dark hair.'

'I'll collect the stuff and let you know when the job's done,' said Moran.

Chapter 21

Pretoria

After speaking to Callard, Weisz instructed a member of staff to check the British Embassy to see if a passport had recently been issued to a white male of Rohm's age. He then phoned Ruth Arnall at Scotland Yard.

'Ruth, Bruce Weisz at the DSO in Pretoria. I've just had a call from Kirsty Callard. She's at home. Andrew Rohm, the guy behind the killing of the four ministers, escaped from Pollsmoor Prison yesterday. She's sure she saw him a couple of hours ago in Knightsbridge.'

'He must have a new identity,' said Arnall, 'and it might be British. It's worth checking on your side if a white male of Rohm's age was recently issued with a British passport.'

'I've put someone on to that,' said Weisz, 'and will get back to you when I hear something.'

'If you get a name we can see if anyone of the same name bought a property in that general area,' said Arnall, 'especially in the last two days. If it was me, I would like to have seen it first. We could also try the hotels. It sounds as if he's staying around there and he's got the money. I'll phone Kirsty and see what more she can tell us. Did Rohm see her, and if he did, would he have recognised her?'

'He looked straight at her,' said Weisz, 'but as to recognition, it's difficult to tell. She thinks he would have recognised her unless he was spaced out. He and another guy gave her a beating before Steiner and I finally nailed him. Let's just say he'd recognise her if she was in disguise. I said I'd ask you to put someone on duty outside her house but she doesn't want it. She's like Steiner. She thinks she can go it alone and doesn't need someone looking after her.'

'That's her choice,' said Arnall, 'and I think Steiner will soon be back. Also, if Rohm wanted to do something nasty, a guard outside the house wouldn't stop him. It's like assassination, and the reason important people are surrounded by layers of security men. I'll let you get going.'

Chapter 22

Shinjuku, Tokyo

At one-thirty in the morning a tall, well-built man left his car in the street and walked to the Hyatt Regency entrance. There were only a few people in the reception area, many in the bars and clubs upstairs. The man went to the lifts. He was carrying a long, slim bag, used for carrying *bokken* and *jo*. He ascended to the seventh floor.

The man left the lift, glanced at the room numbers, and walked along the passage to room 773. He stopped outside, sliding a baseball bat from his bag. He listened, inserted a plastic key into the lock and eased the door open. There was still no sound and he entered.

Steiner was lying asleep on his back in the double bed, the quilt covering only the lower half of his body. As the man positioned himself on one side of the bed, Steiner opened his eyes. But it was too late, and before he could move and deflect what was coming, the man struck him with force on his solar plexus, the mass of nerve cells in the upper abdomen, causing an involuntary lifting of his head and an immediate loss of consciousness.

With muted, brutal strikes the man lifted and rained the heavy bat on Steiner's chest, legs and arms, beating rhythmically in concert, deliberately avoiding Steiner's head. After a ten-second onslaught he lowered his bat. He had done enough, and stepped back, surveying his work. He hadn't given anyone such a beating for a long time and Steiner was lucky he was in good condition. He took a note typed on an A4 sheet of paper and a JAL flight ticket to London Heathrow made out to James Steiner from his jacket pocket and placed it on top of Steiner's unconscious, supine form. He returned his bat to the slim bag and left the room, closing the door quietly behind them. When he reached his car, he sped from the scene.

Chapter 23

Chiyoda, Tokyo

'Did he leave the message and the ticket?' said Kitamura into the phone. It was thirty minutes after Steiner had received the beating.

'As instructed,' said David Tate. 'It was perfect, and Steiner didn't have a chance. He was unconscious but will come round. If he's smart he'll be on the 0600 flight to Heathrow.'

'Excellent,' said Kitamura. 'Do you think Steiner saw his assailant?' Kitamura was happy not to know the man's identity. It was better that way, unless identification was necessary.

'I don't think so,' said Tate. 'He was hit as he opened his eyes, and if anything, he'd only have got a faint impression, nothing that would excite an identity parade. Anyway, he wouldn't have known the person. He and his people won't even know it came from you. It could have been any one of your associates who dislikes interference in Japanese affairs.'

'You sum it up very well,' said Kitamura. 'I'll see you and the others later. Make sure you check he's on the flight and let me know.'

'We'll be at the gate,' said Tate.

Chapter 24

Hyatt Regency Hotel, Shinjuku, Tokyo

Thirty minutes after the man left the hotel, Steiner regained consciousness. The pain across his body was acute. He was visibly bruised on his chest and legs with blue welts, but bones hadn't been broken or skin perforated and there was no bleeding. He rolled sideways to the edge of the bed and then onto the floor, landing on his knees. His thoughts were clear, and he was glad he had not been struck on the head. The wounds would heal and he could move. He was annoyed he had not sensed the man's presence earlier. He noticed the sheet of paper, with the airline ticket attached, and picked it up. It read:

Leave on the 0600 JAL flight from Narita to London Heathrow this Friday. You'll be killed if you don't leave on the flight, return to Japan or interfere further in affairs that don't concern you. This time you were lucky.

Steiner checked the ticket. It had his name on it. He got slowly to his feet and sat on the bed, casting his thoughts back to the assault. He remembered the figure of a man with a raised baseball bat at the side of the bed, but in the split second after opening his eyes and losing consciousness, he hadn't seen enough of the man's face to identify him. It was two-fifteen and he went over to the phone. Chinen had said he should only trust Arnall, but he decided he had to include Shimada this time. The man had to be working for Kitamura. How had they found out he was in Tokyo? He dialled Shimada's home number and he answered.

'Shimada *san*, James Steiner. I'm sorry to ring you

so late. I've been attacked in my room at the hotel.'

'Are you alright?' said Shimada tersely.

'Yes,' said Steiner. 'I think there was only one and he caught me asleep in bed. I sensed something, but I was too late. I recall seeing a man with a bat and that was it. His face was shielded by his arm. He gave me a beating but it was a warning. He avoided my head. This was confirmed by a note he left. I'll read it to you.' Steiner read out the message and when he'd finished said: 'The ticket is attached.'

'I didn't think this would happen,' said Shimada. 'Kitamura's well informed and wants to make his mark before you move. What are you going to do? I think you should phone Ruth Arnall.'

'I'll phone her now,' said Steiner, 'but I won't be returning on that flight. Kitamura has revealed his guilt and made me more determined to take him back to London, exactly the opposite of what he wanted. We'll proceed as discussed but I can't stay here. His people will be watching the airport and if I don't fly they'll come after me. They have no intention of letting me near Kitamura and if they get me this time it will be my end.'

'They might not only wait at Narita to see if you leave,' said Shimada. 'They could be watching the hotel even now and waiting. They'd then follow you.'

'If I'm to get Kitamura I have to leave now,' said Steiner, 'and it'll mean going to another hotel without the chance of being seen. Is there any way you can help me get out through a back entrance?'

'This is what I'll do,' said Shimada. 'I'll speak to the hotel and meet you at the bottom of the fire escape. There's one at the end of your passage. We'll go out through a rear exit. The chances of these people watching all exits are small, and I don't think they'd choose them over the main entrance. If they manage to tail us, we'll soon find out at this time of night, and I'll have them stopped until we're clear. We'll go to the Hilton Hotel. It's nearby.'

'Let's do it,' said Steiner. 'When can you be here?'

'Twenty minutes,' said Shimada.

'Thank you,' said Steiner. 'It gives me time to ring Arnall.' He cut the call, checked his contact list and dialled Ruth Arnall's direct number.

'Ruth, James Steiner. I'm at the hotel in Tokyo. Kitamura's on to me.'

'James, what do you mean?' said Arnall. 'You've only just got there.'

Steiner told her what had taken place and the gist of his conversation with Shimada. 'I'm meeting him at the fire exit in fifteen minutes.'

'Are you sure you want to go ahead?' said Arnall, feeling obliged to ask the question. 'I wouldn't blame you for returning and forgetting the whole business.'

'I'm sure,' said Steiner. 'I've lost the element of surprise, but for me, Kitamura's guilt is confirmed. When I don't catch the flight they'll intensify their guard and do what they can to find me, but I'll get through. I'm here now and I'm going to his estate near Oku-Nikko to get him. He's going there later today. The big question is how did they know?'

'I'm as much in the dark as you,' said Arnall. 'If I didn't completely trust the three officers you met to keep quiet, I wouldn't have told them about you and let them in on my plan. They are also useful as devil's advocates.'

'What about the assistant commissioner?' said Steiner.

'I'm confident it hasn't gone past him,' said Arnall.

'Then that leaves the Japanese,' said Steiner. 'I trust Shimada now that I've met him and he has told me that only his boss, the superintendent general of the MPD, and a deputy know of this. But, it's a fact of life that those you feel you can trust sometimes end up betraying you.'

'You've also noticed that,' said Arnall. 'Trust and betrayal are forever the drivers in love and war, business and pleasure. Please keep in contact. I can't help worrying about you and this makes it worse.'

'I can look after myself,' said Steiner. 'Kitamura and his mates are not the first who have taken a dislike to me. There is one other thing. I asked Shimada to speak to you and get a DNA profile of the blood on the knife sent to him. We might be able to get hold of Kitamura's DNA over here and compare it. It's conceivable that one of his men, Tate, Norman or Oda, seen with him in London and now with him here, could have killed the girl.' He briefly told her what Shimada had said about the martial arts school on the estate.

'Shimada hasn't asked, but I'll send the sample,' said Arnall. 'You're right. It might save us a lot of time and avoid embarrassment, but if they are guilty, they were acting on his behalf, and he is equally guilty. Now I must let you go.'

Steiner replaced the phone, collected his bag and left the room. He could feel the aching in his body but knew the best way to get over it was to purge it from his mind.

There was no one in the passage and when he reached the fire escape, he descended to the ground floor. Shimada was waiting for him.

'Put these on and come this way,' said Shimada, holding out a white cotton coat and a wide felt hat. 'Hang your head and apart from your height you'll look like one of the staff. I'll take your bag.'

Steiner put on the coat and hat and followed Shimada. He led the way through the kitchen to a rear door that opened onto a long alley. They went down it into the street, a block along from the main hotel entrance, and to Shimada's car. There were the usual number of parked cars and, other than the odd passing vehicle, the street was quiet.

'We'll see if they're looking out for us when we get going,' said Shimada, starting the engine. He drew away from the kerb and drove along the long street towards the station. Near the end of the street he turned abruptly into a side street and stopped between two cars. 'I'll give it a minute.'

No other car entered the street, and after two minutes, Shimada pulled away. He drove to the next main street and turned left towards the Hilton Hotel. When he neared it, he parked a short distance from the entrance. 'It's so close to the Hyatt Regency we could easily have walked,' he said. 'We're ahead of the pack and if they're keeping watch they're still outside the other place.'

They entered the hotel and without checking in, Shimada led the way to the lifts and up to room 213. 'Hope sweet home, James *san*,' he said. 'I hope you're not going to cause any more trouble.'

'I'll try and keep you out of it,' said Steiner. 'Is our meeting with Maruyama still on?'

'I've been thinking about that,' said Shimada. 'If this person knew about you then those behind him could know about me and put a tail on me. They probably haven't yet done it, hoping the beating would be enough, but when they find you're not on the plane and have disappeared they might, and we can't take the risk. I could speak to you on the phone and send what I've got by fax but it is better that we meet. I doubt they know about Maruyama and I'll send him to the hotel at noon. By then we should have news on Kitamura's movements. He'll be at the estate for a week and you've got time. I think you should rest now and give

82

your body a chance to recover. Ring me when you get up.' He bowed and left the room.

Steiner made some green tea. He thought about the night's events and whether he should tell Kirsty. She wouldn't like it if he didn't and the inflictions were not serious. He dialled her number and she answered.

'Kirsty, it's James...'

'You've been clubbing with Shimada,' said Callard before he could continue. 'It's three in the morning over there.'

'It wasn't as pleasant as that,' said Steiner. He told her what had happened. 'It could have been a lot worse if he'd gone for my head and let his enthusiasm exceed his instructions. Kitamura simply wants me and the Met to leave him alone without resorting to anything too heavy. But if I don't leave and he catches me going for him, he won't hesitate in killing me.'

'And you've decided to stay and carry on,' said Kirsty. 'I think you should get out now and leave the police with their resources and methods to sort it out.'

'It's not in me to do that,' said Steiner, 'and I know what I'm up against. I'm not pulling out on Arnall. You must learn to believe in me.'

'I do believe in you,' said Callard, 'but I also love you. You're in great danger, more than you've ever been in before. Rohm only sent one man, Kallis, after you. Kitamura is a completely different story with thugs like Tate, Norman and Oda. And this time you'll be going into their territory. I'd like you to scan and send to me by email the map and other details Shimada gives you about Kitamura. I'd then have some idea what you're up against and it would make me feel a lot better.'

'I don't see how it'll help,' said Steiner, 'but I'll send it to you. Arnall will also be in close contact with me.'

'I'm aware of that,' said Kirsty, 'but I don't intend to start bleeping her for information. I want to know as much as she does.'

'You'll have the stuff tomorrow before I leave,' said Steiner.

Kirsty paused before saying: 'I was going to keep this until you got back. I saw Andrew Rohm on the corner of Montpelier Street near Harrods. I phoned Bruce Weisz and he told me Rohm escaped on Wednesday afternoon. He was being taken to the law courts from the jail.' She relayed the conversation she'd had with Weisz. 'There was no point in telling you and distracting you from the job over there.'

'I want you to stay in a hotel until I return,' said Steiner. 'Weisz should have told you to leave the house. There's a hotel opposite the V&A. I think it's the Rembrandt.'

'I know the one you mean,' said Kirsty, feeling foolish. She could do nothing if Rohm and his men came for her.

'I want you to do it now,' said Steiner. 'If he saw you, and I think he did, he'll move very quickly to remove you. You'd be a threat. I'd return now but guys like that don't hang around when their security is threatened.'

'I'll move to the hotel in the morning,' said Kirsty. 'It's late now. Don't fret about me. Concentrate on Kitamura. I love you, James.'

'I love you too.' Steiner replaced the receiver. Rohm's escape had unnerved him more than he'd let on to Kirsty, but was glad she'd told him. He could now think about Kitamura. She'd be safe until he got back. He went to bed. His strength was returning and sleep was a vital part of recovery.

Chapter 25

Chiyoda, Tokyo

'Are you absolutely sure he didn't get on the plane?' said Kitamura. It was six in the morning and he was talking to Tate on his home phone.

'Yes,' said Tate. 'Oda and I were outside immigration at Narita three hours before the flight. But that's not all. Norman was also at the hotel and when we told him he spoke to the receptionist. Steiner's checked out.'

'Did anyone see him book out?' said Kitamura.

'It was done early this morning,' said Oda, 'and by a Japanese. His bags were also removed. He's gone to ground and that means he's still after you.'

'I wanted to leave for the estate at five this afternoon but I'll delay it,' said Kitamura. 'You, Norman and Oda come to my flat now. I don't think Steiner will try anything in Tokyo. He'll try my estate and I want to be ready for him.'

'What do you intend to do?' said Tate. 'He could be on his way there now. Perhaps you should stay in Tokyo.'

'And go into hiding?' said Kitamura. 'I'll never do that. No, we'll be prepared when he announces himself at the estate. Steiner's contact in Tokyo is a senior officer in the MPD, a man named Kenichi Shimada. I want him picked up and taken to Oku-Nikko. He could be useful to me. He must have an idea of Steiner's moves and probably helped him get out of the hotel to a resting place. He lives in Kichijoji, a smart neighbourhood fifteen minutes west of Shinjuku by car.' Kitamura found Shimada's home address and repeated it to Tate. 'If you move quickly you'll find him there now. I'll wait in Tokyo until you pick him

85

up.'

'I'll get onto it,' said Tate. 'I think you should wait in Tokyo until we've got him and taken him to the estate. We'll be waiting when you arrive.'

'I agree,' said Kitamura. 'I'll be here at my flat.' He terminated the call. After digesting what he had heard, he looked at his watch and then phoned Rohm at his hotel. It was ten o'clock in London. Rohm answered.

'Andrew, Shingen Kitamura. I've just had news about Steiner.'

'I hope it's good,' said Rohm. 'Let me have it.'

'He was given a beating in his hotel room a few hours ago,' said Kitamura, 'and a message left telling him to be on the 0600 flight to Heathrow.'

'And he didn't show at Narita,' said Rohm.

'You're right,' said Kitamura. 'He's also checked out of the hotel. It was done for him and he's disappeared.'

'I'm sure you can guess where he's going,' said Rohm. 'I didn't think he'd be deterred short of killing him. Steiner will not stop until he gets what he wants. He is extremely dangerous and won't try for you in Tokyo. That means your estate, and I think he's going there now. He is unpredictable and you'll never know what he's planning until he suddenly appears. When you think he's given up he will be in your face.'

'I'm learning,' said Kitamura, 'and I've already taken steps to secure an advantage. My men are pulling in Shimada, the Japanese police superintendent who has been working with Scotland Yard, and taking him to the estate. I'll grill him when I get there later. We'll be prepared for Steiner.'

'I wish you luck,' said Rohm. 'I'll believe he's no longer a threat when he's dead.'

After a moment's thought, Kitamura phoned a number in London. A man answered. 'It's Shingen

Kitamura. This might be too soon for you to know anything but Steiner has gone to ground.'

'What do you mean?' said the man. 'He was at the Hyatt Regency Hotel in Shinjuku.'

'He was given a beating in his room with instructions to return to London,' said Kitamura. 'The flight was at 0600 from Narita and he was not on it. He has also checked out of the hotel.'

'That's not good,' said the man. 'He's now dangerous because he knows you're on to him. He might have phoned Arnall. I'll see if she's heard from him. What are you going to do about it, if anything?'

'I'm getting hold of Shimada,' said Kitamura, 'and having him taken to the estate. He must know something.'

'Isn't that too much of a risk?' said the man. 'The last thing you want is to be caught snatching a senior police officer. You'd never be able to prove he was linked to a plot to take you back to England, and without that, you'd show your hand unnecessarily.'

'No one would know,' said Kitamura, 'and it's a risk I'm prepared to take if it means removing Steiner. Let me know if you hear anything. Steiner's probably so arrogant he'll go it alone and not tell anyone.'

'You'll hear from me either way,' said the man.

Chapter 26

Kichijoji, Tokyo

When Shimada received the call from Steiner and heard about the assault on him, he was unnerved. He did not doubt Kitamura was behind it, and if the man had knowledge of Steiner's whereabouts, then there was a very good chance he also knew of Shimada's involvement in the plan to take him back to London. Shimada lived alone in Kichijoji, and when he got back to his house, he had decided he could do little else other than be vigilant. The case hadn't taken up much of his time and there were a number of cases that needed urgent attention. The only thing now was to brief Maruyama later about the meeting with Steiner at the hotel. After that it was up to Steiner, and he'd be either successful and cart Kitamura back to England, or fail and be killed. He didn't think Steiner would have the freedom and time to get a sample from Kitamura to compare with the DNA sample he wanted from Arnall.

Shimada slept until six, the morning still dark. He was about to get up and leave for work when he heard a faint noise in the passage outside his room. It was not repeated, and, believing he must have been mistaken, Shimada got up, slipped on his gown and went to the door. He slid the screen open and stepped through.

The move was swift, and Shimada's only sight of his assailant told him it was a man he had never seen before. With the dexterity of a cat, the man grabbed Shimada's shoulder and spun him round, delivering a savage blow with the edge of his hand to the jugular. A second man appeared, and Shimada was unconscious before he started to fall. His assailant lifted and draped him over his shoulder. The men did not speak as they went down the passage and through the rear door of the house into the alley at the side, vanishing from the scene and leaving only silence to greet the first shimmer of dawn.

Chapter 27

Shinjuku, Tokyo

Steiner was in his hotel room, and at twelve-thirty, when Maruyama had not appeared, he phoned Shimada. A woman answered and after she told him Shimada had not turned up at work, he asked to speak to Maruyama. He was put through.

'Maruyama *san*, James Steiner. I tried Shimada *san* but he's not there. He said you would meet me at the hotel thirty minutes ago.'

'I am very sorry, Steiner *san*,' said Maruyama. 'Shimada is not here and hasn't told me to meet you. We rang him at home and on his cellphone but there's no answer.'

'When did you last speak to him?' said Steiner.

'Yesterday,' said Maruyama, 'after he'd seen you.'

'Then you don't know I was given a beating last night in my hotel room,' said Steiner. 'I called Shimada and he helped me move to another hotel.'

'So Kitamura is onto you,' said Maruyama. 'He could be onto us and that might explain Shimada's absence.'

'Shimada thought the same,' said Steiner, 'except that he felt your involvement in this case was not known. For that reason he was going to ask you to meet me. You were to bring me the information on Kitamura so I could get moving this afternoon. I was also going to get a car and some other items.'

'I've already got what you want,' said Maruyama. 'If that's what Shimada agreed, I'll come to your hotel. I can be there in an hour and I'll bring the car.'

'That's what Shimada agreed,' said Steiner. 'I'm in room 213 at the Hilton Hotel.'

Thirty minutes later, Maruyama knocked on the

door and Steiner let him in. He was carrying a soft, black bag and seated himself. 'The car's at the back of the hotel,' he said, placing a ring of keys on the table. 'It's a silver Lexus saloon. The number's on the ring.'

'Thank you,' said Steiner. 'You've got something else.'

Maruyama unzipped the bag and removed the contents, a plastic folder, binoculars, heavy-duty binding tape and a pack of surgical gloves. He opened the folder. 'There's a map and a layout of the estate and local area. It shows the period house and surrounding buildings, including the training school and dormitory, and the museum. The grounds cover five acres and form a series of traditional Japanese gardens, linked by bridges over pools of water stocked with carp and supplied by small falls. There's also a secluded *zen* garden near the house with raked gravel and rocks, quiescent and perfect for meditation. I've heard it is all very beautiful.'

'I'm sure it is,' said Steiner, 'and Kitamura can afford it. Where is the *ryokan*?'

Maruyama pointed to the layout. 'Here, two kilometres to the south of the estate and connected to it by a narrow road. The estate is surrounded by a six-foot stone wall capped with an apex of tiles and iron gates at the entrance. There are usually two guards on the gate but sometimes, for whatever reason, no one is on duty. There appears to be no set time and it is random. They might be watching the gates from inside the wall.'

'What's the *ryokan* doing there?' said Steiner looking at the map. 'It's in the middle of nowhere. Who'd want to stay in it? If I stay there tonight, I'd be too obvious.'

'It is on the edge of the national park,' said Maruyama, 'and people like it because it is so isolated. There are thirty rooms, most of them booked at this time of the year when the autumn colours are at their most beautiful. I don't think you will stand out because foreigners frequently stay there and I've reserved a room for you in case you need it. You might want to stay there tonight.'

'I'll decide when I get to the area,' said Steiner. 'I want to get this business over with and it'll probably mean working at night. What about Kitamura's movements? Who's with him when he's there?'

'When he is not with the guys in the school and showing people the collection in his museum, he keeps very much to himself in the house,' said Maruyama. 'It is 300 years old with many rooms, old *tatami* and wooden floors. He never has anyone on call or a guard present, but that might have changed since your arrival.'

'And he has no wife, children?' said Steiner. 'What about a mistress?'

'I was coming to that,' said Maruyama. 'He's divorced and his ex-wife and two children live in Tokyo. The children seldom visit the estate. He has a mistress, Akiko, and she has been seen on the estate. She has a flat in Tokyo. I don't know if she's there now.'

Steiner nodded slowly. 'I could do without her.'

'When are you leaving?' said Maruyama. 'After speaking to you I contacted Kitamura's office for an update on his movements. He's leaving for the estate later this afternoon as we expected.' Maruyama looked at the map. 'It is five hours from here to Numata and another hour to Kamata where the road forks, to the north and to the east and the Konsei pass. The *ryokan* is forty-five minutes on the north fork. I've marked the route on the map.'

'It all adds up,' said Steiner. 'I'm leaving when you go and will head for the area. I'll probably rest up in the

92

ryokan and then go to the estate. My plan then depends on what I see. I don't intend hanging around waiting for the ideal moment.'

'I'm sorry you can't speak to Shimada before you go,' said Maruyama. 'It's very strange, his disappearing like that.'

'I won't say what I'm thinking except that I don't like it,' said Steiner. 'When he appears, tell him I'll call when I've got Kitamura and ready to leave. Shimada might not have told you, but I asked him to tell Ruth Arnall to send over a sample of the DNA found on the knife that killed the girl. He hadn't told her when I spoke to her early this morning, but she'll see it's done. I want a comparison made with a sample I'll take from Kitamura before I leave. At the moment that means coming to Tokyo and bringing Kitamura with me. A friend in Tokyo will help me. If I get a perfect match, Arnall will fix the flight.'

'I understand and will wait for your call,' said Maruyama. 'Good luck James *san*. You'll be doing us a favour.'

'Thank you for your help,' said Steiner. They bowed and Maruyama left the room.

For a while Steiner studied the map Maruyama had given him. He knew Nikko fairly well up to the Konsei Pass, but was not familiar with Oku-Nikko and noticed that the estate was partly bordered by the Ozegahara Marsh to the south and west, something he didn't like. He thought about going directly to the estate tonight, taking a calculated chance at where Kitamura might be, and making a move on him, but decided it was being too ambitious, and instead a brief look at the place after he'd stopped at the *ryokan* would suffice. He had time on his side and didn't want to screw up when it could have been avoided by being more careful. That meant staying in the *ryokan* as planned, but, whatever

Maruyama had said, Steiner didn't like the idea. The place was close to the estate and there had to be the chance, however slim, of word being passed on that a foreigner of his description was staying there. But it was this close proximity that was an advantage, and he didn't intend to stay there for more than one night. If he couldn't get Kitamura by the end of tomorrow, he would find a place to sleep in Kamata.

Steiner thought again about the job itself: getting hold of Kitamura. He couldn't see himself doing that anywhere other than inside the house when ideally he'd be alone. If there was a guard present, he'd either have to remove him or wait until he left his post, if there was an indication he would. In the end, successful execution of the job would depend on intuition and judiciously assessing the situation as it presented itself.

Then there was the final part of the job: leaving the area with Kitamura. The decision was where to leave the car, and that could only be made when he got there. He would want the Lexus as close as possible to the estate to avoid spending excessive time leading Kitamura to it afterwards and prevent it from being seen while he was on the job. A swift getaway was important and might even be critical if others had been alerted.

Steiner left his hotel room with his bag shortly after two o'clock. He went out through the back of the building and located the car. He got in, adjusted the seat and mirror, left the car park and joined the motorway heading north-west for Numata.

Chapter 28

Knightsbridge, London SW7

At precisely three in the morning, Phillip Moran pulled into the car park behind the Brompton Oratory. Across the lawn and on the other side of a stone wall was Ennismore Garden Mews. There was no one about, and for a while he studied the setting. He went slowly to the narrow lane, along it to the mews, and then to number 32, the address given to him by Levy and a house of two storeys. There were no lights on inside and he tried the door. It was fitted with a mortise and Yale locks, and, as expected, it did not yield, except that a slight but noticeable movement of the door when he pressed against the mortise indicated it was not engaged. He extracted two slim tools from his pocket, a tension wrench and hook pick. After aligning the pins inside the lock cylinder, he turned the wrench, opened the door and entered the house, finding himself in a standard hall with doors to two rooms, a passage to the kitchen and stairs to the first floor.

Moran was still, and then climbed the stairs to the landing. There were three doors going from it, a bathroom, a vacant double bedroom and a room with a closed door. He went to it, turned the handle and entered.

Kirsty Callard was unmistakeable, lying asleep on her back in the bed, half-covered by a top sheet. When he reached her side, he placed his hand over her mouth and said: 'Kirsty.'

Kirsty opened her eyes wide. She stared at him, moving pithily against his hand, but she quickly assimilated the situation and stayed quiet. He moved his hand an inch from her mouth and said: 'Shut up and listen. You're coming with me. I won't harm you if you do as you're told.'

'What do you want?' she said softly. 'Who are you? I don't know you.'

Moran hadn't bothered to cover his head because he didn't think Levy's client would let her live. It was the tone in Levy's voice. 'You don't have to,' he said. He pulled away the sheet, momentarily feasting his eyes on her half-naked body. 'Get up and put some clothes on. We're going for a drive.'

She'd been through this before. There was no option and pointless resisting. 'Where're we going? My boyfriend will be back at any moment.'

He pulled her up off the bed and onto her feet. 'He won't,' he said, 'unless he left Japan for London nine hours ago. I assume the one I'm referring to is your boyfriend. Now get dressed.'

Kirsty went to a cupboard and with him staring at her, put on a white shirt, denim jeans and flat shoes. She stuffed some clothes into a bag and faced him. 'I'll need some things from the bathroom. When am I coming back? Who said my boyfriend's in Japan? They're mistaken. Why do you want me?'

'They're not the kind who make mistakes,' said Moran. 'Your boyfriend's there and you might have recognised someone in the street. He's only taking precautions.'

Kirsty was stunned by what she heard and looked away. James was right. Rohm had moved quickly. But how did Moran know James was in Japan? It was too much of a coincidence for him to be working for two separate people.

Moran moved to the door. 'Get your stuff from the bathroom. I want to get going.'

Taking her bag, Kirsty walked past him to the bathroom. He followed her and watched as she placed items into a bag. When she'd finished he pointed to the stairs. 'Good, let's go. I'm glad you didn't try and take anything else.'

Moran led the way down the stairs to the front door. He opened it, checked to see if there was anyone about and when he saw it was clear pushed her out onto the cobbled street. He closed the door, took her by the arm and led her down the lane and to the car. When they got there, he ushered her in through the driver's door to the passenger seat and got in. He gunned the engine, drove down the driveway and into the Brompton Road. He turned right, joined the Fulham Road, and sped down it through four sets of traffic lights until he came to Gilston Road. He went up it and stopped outside a three-storey Victorian house. He glanced at Kirsty. 'This is not Knightsbridge but it's still pricey.'

Moran got out of the car, walked round, opened the passenger door and led Kirsty out. She followed him to the door and through into the house. He led the way up the stairs to one of two bedrooms on the second floor, a standard mortise lock on the door. The room was en-suite with a shower, toilet and basin and furnished with a bed, chair and dressing table. There were wall lights and central heating. The only external light was from a skylight in the ceiling.

'I'll be back in a few hours,' said Moran. 'There's no way out. If you scream, no one will hear you.' He left the room, locked the door and went down the stairs.

Kirsty sat on the bed, slowly recovering from the shock of being pulled out of her bed by one of Rohm's thugs. She was angry that she'd not heeded Steiner's words that Rohm would move quickly, and that the chance he'd seen her was very real. He'd been staring straight at her, and only someone totally unaware of what was going on around them would have failed to recognize a person they'd so badly wanted to kill, even if preoccupied by something else. As she thought about it, the more certain she became that Rohm would kill her. The fact that Moran had not cared to hide his features was testimony to that. Rohm was biding his time, because with her locked up and out of the way, there was no urgency, and he probably had other things to clear up first, having just arrived in London.

Kirsty looked round the room. She had to escape, but the only way was through the door. She'd heard the lock being engaged and the bolts slammed shut and she couldn't open it on her own; it could only be when Moran returned. But he had not been chosen for the job for nothing and would not easily be caught unawares. She thought about the things Steiner had taught her: overcoming a antagonist was primarily about mental calm and staying cool, relaxing completely so as not to cramp your freedom of movement, and allowing intuition to control the action – conscious thought was restrictive. She had no formal training in combat techniques but that was not necessary. Any technique, however crude or unrefined, was perfect if it produced the desired result, in this case the subjugation of Moran. If one is not as strong as the opponent physically, one has to attack painful, vulnerable parts that cause the most pain and at least temporary immobilisation. She knew what she had to do and she could only wait for Moran's return. She lay on the bed, hoping to get some sleep.

Chapter 29

New Scotland Yard, London SW1

'Late yesterday London time a man gave Steiner a hiding in his hotel,' said Ruth Arnall. 'He phoned me shortly after it happened, around three o'clock in the morning their time.' She was in her office with Dance, Mercer and Easter, and related what Steiner had told her about the attack, and that a message and ticket had been left instructing him to leave Japan. 'I don't think it'll be a surprise when I tell you he has no intention of being on the plane. Shimada was going to help him relocate to the Hilton Hotel. Kitamura is clearly behind it and someone must have told him Steiner was in town and they knew where to find him.'

'Well it's not from here,' said Dance. 'We're the only ones who know and I hope Steiner doesn't suspect us.'

'He gave it as a possibility, but he doesn't know you as well as I do,' said Arnall. 'I told him the three of you have my complete trust and confidence and that a leak could only have come from the Japanese, unintentionally or intentionally, however you want to describe innocence or collaborating with the enemy.'

'I'm glad we're clear on that,' said Easter. 'No one outside this room knows anything about Steiner, let alone that he's in Tokyo trying to grab Kitamura. If he's staying put, I assume he's still going after the man and not going back to full-time karate training.'

'He's had all the training he needs,' said Arnall, 'and I believe if anything it's others who want him to teach them. Your assumption is correct. He is not giving up on Kitamura and he's going to his estate on the edge of Oku-Nikko to get him. He's probably on his way there as we speak. There are two other things.

First, Steiner wants a sample of the DNA on the knife sent to Shimada. There is the chance one of Kitamura's men killed Brit, and we don't want Steiner to bring back the wrong man. I was sure it was Kitamura, but even if it's not, he has to be behind it, and that means guilt by association.'

'And Steiner will get a match with Kitamura's DNA before he brings him back,' said Dance. 'That makes it more difficult. What if he manages to get a match and the DNA samples are not the same?'

'We'll decide that later,' said Arnall. 'If it's not a perfect match, I'll have to ask Steiner to find the real killer. If it's not one of Kitamura's henchmen – the three with him in London – then it's someone we don't know about. We'd then be back to square one.'

'What's the second thing?' said Easter.

'Late yesterday afternoon I had a call from Bruce Weisz of South Africa's DSO,' said Arnall. 'He'd just spoken to Kirsty Callard, Steiner's girlfriend, on the phone. She's sure she saw a man, Andrew Rohm, near Harrods. Steiner helped put Rohm inside for life six weeks ago. Weisz confirmed Rohm had escaped from Pollsmoor Prison in Cape Town on Wednesday. Rohm is British and it's likely he's travelling on a British passport under a new identity. Weisz is checking the British Embassy in South Africa.'

'I can't see how it affects us,' said Mercer.

'It doesn't affect this case directly,' said Arnall, 'but it might draw attention to Steiner when he returns, something we don't want when the fewer who know about his trip to Japan the better. When I say Steiner helped put Rohm behind bars, it is putting it mildly. He was the agent, working alone and independently, who nailed Rohm, the national director of public prosecutions, Paul Bale, and other prominent figures for direct involvement in serious and organised crime.

Rohm hates Steiner's guts, and if he hears where he is and that he is trying to pull in a Japanese cabinet minister, possibly a future prime minister, it will run through the media like a virus and damage us. For this reason, I'll be doing what I can to find Rohm under his new identity and get him locked up. I think Weisz will be coming over here to help where he can.'

'Who will you get to go after Rohm?' said Mercer. 'If you're not careful, they might find out about Steiner and then about this job in Japan. Why, for example, did Weisz contact you and not someone else in the Met? Does Weisz know Steiner's on this job in Japan?'

'You're right,' said Arnall, 'and I'll wait until we hear more from Steiner. I didn't confirm it with Weisz but I think Steiner would have told him I've taken him on. I asked Weisz about Steiner in the first place because I'd heard about this guy who'd pulled in Rohm and his mates and had lived in Japan studying the martial arts. I thought that type of training might be useful. I can easily explain my delay to Weisz if he asks and I might ask him to contact the Met separately about Rohm. He would have done that as routine procedure anyway if he'd not heard from Kirsty.'

'I didn't know Weisz was in on it at the start,' said Dance. 'So he probably knows about Steiner's involvement in all this. I hope he hasn't told his people over there.'

'I'm sure he hasn't,' said Arnall. 'He knows it is sensitive.'

'Does Weisz know you're doing this without authorisation?' said Mercer.

'He certainly doesn't know,' said Arnall, 'and neither does Steiner. Both would have recoiled in horror if they had known. Nothing is perfect and sometimes it is necessary not to reveal all when you want to get the job done.'

'Weisz might not have liked it, but I wouldn't be so sure about Steiner,' said Dance. 'I think he has his own rules and code of morality.'

'And we carry on as usual,' said Easter.

'Yes,' said Arnall. 'I'll keep you informed about Steiner's movements.'

Chapter 30

Mount Street, Mayfair, London W1

'Moran collected Kirsty last night and took her to the place in South Kensington,' said Peter Levy. He was on the phone to Rohm at the hotel. 'He'll go and see her this morning. What do you want me to do with her?'

'I'll decide when I find out what's happening with Steiner in Japan,' said Rohm. 'Make sure Moran looks after her. I don't want any complaints. I'll ring you later.'

Chapter 31

Chelsea, London SW3

'I hear your people gave Steiner a thrashing in his hotel,' said the man. He had just reached Kitamura at his flat. 'He seems to have recovered and doesn't intend to leave Japan. He won't give up on you.'

'I know that,' said Kitamura. 'He was given the treatment early this morning when he lay in bed. He was left instructions to leave Japan at 0600 but didn't show. Do you know where he is? It doesn't really bother me because I'm sure he's going to the estate. That's where I want him, on my own soil.'

The man wasn't surprised. 'I believe he was taken to the Hilton Hotel by Shimada. Arnall also believes he's heading for your estate.'

'I've already collected Shimada,' said Kitamura. 'He's waiting for me at the estate. I'm leaving after this call. I'll see what he can tell me and then get rid of him. Even if Steiner was taken to the Hilton, he won't stay there long. He's probably on his way to the estate as we speak.'

'There's something else from Arnall,' said the man. 'When I told you Steiner had worked for the DSO in South Africa, and had been responsible for jailing men who'd killed the four South African government ministers, you said one of them was a close friend of yours. Steiner has a woman in London, Kirsty Callard, and yesterday she saw one of those men, Andrew Rohm, outside Harrods in West London. She immediately phoned Bruce Weisz of the DSO in Pretoria and he confirmed that Rohm had escaped yesterday afternoon from Pollsmoor Prison in Cape Town. Was Rohm the guy you were referring to?'

'Yes, I spoke to him yesterday morning. He told me

he'd escaped and was in London. This is not good news. The fact she recognised him and told the DSO means they'll be after him like a pack of starving dogs. I'll phone Rohm now and see if he's aware of this. He might have seen her. It would be ironic and a cruel fate if Rohm was sent back to jail because Steiner's woman, of all people, happened to spot him in the street. I'm really glad you told me. We might need your assistance in this.'

'I'll do what I can as long as I'm not exposed,' said the man. 'You must never reveal my name to Rohm. If he's caught, and for whatever reason spills the beans on us, it will bring us down faster than jumping out of a plane without a chute. It's worth remembering that the DSO would have contacted Interpol or the Met in due course about Rohm's escape. Also, it appears that Weisz doesn't know Arnall brought on Steiner without authorisation.'

'Do you regret not exposing Arnall's plan to bring in an outsider and go after me when you first heard about it?' said Kitamura. 'Unless you're very clever, it's too late now. Your career would go down the tube and you'd risk being associated with me.'

'I don't regret it,' said the man. 'She chose to act secretly without authorisation and I decided to let her stew in her own juice. She's a law unto herself and needs to understand her position in the Met. I don't believe Steiner's got a chance in hell of bringing you back to this country, and ultimately Arnall's little empire will collapse around her. I can see her being thrown out of the Met and possibly facing charges.'

'That could only happen if her little scheme is exposed,' said Kitamura. 'And, you can't do that now without placing yourself in an extremely invidious position. Steiner will never get me and if I don't kill him without leaving a trace the only way Arnall could be exposed is by his returning to England and shouting his mouth off. I'm confident Steiner will never leave Japan and never be found. As regards Arnall, you might just have to be content with the fact that her plan failed.'

'That would be enough for me,' said the man. 'I'll contact you when I hear more. Let me know how you get on with Shimada and Steiner.'

Chapter 32

Chiyoda, Tokyo

After the call from London, Kitamura phoned Andrew Rohm on his mobile. Rohm answered.

'Andrew, Kitamura. I'm in Tokyo. Where are you? Have you left the hotel?'

'Yes,' said Rohm. 'I'm in my new house. It's in Belgravia. How are things going?'

'I've just had a call from my friend in London,' said Kitamura. 'You won't like hearing this, but he told me Steiner's girlfriend in London spotted you near Harrods. She had your escape confirmed by a guy named Bruce Weisz of the DSO in Pretoria and he told Ruth Arnall at the Met, the one who's after me.'

'That's what I didn't want,' said Rohm. 'I thought Kirsty might have seen me, but couldn't take the chance and had her taken in last night. If she had recognised me I hoped she hadn't made contact with the law, but she moved quickly. There's nothing more I can do, and I think the police will have difficulty finding me under my new identity. I might at some stage have to go under the knife but I want to avoid it if I can. I'll just have to be careful and hope they don't get a lucky break. I have always been aware that Interpol and the Met would in due course be notified of my escape.'

'There is some consolation,' said Kitamura. 'Arnall is going to delay doing anything about chasing after you because it might expose the fact that she hired Steiner to go after me without authorisation. She got Steiner's name from Weisz, who she'd met previously, because she heard some guy had done a good job in having you and your colleagues arrested. Weisz might be satisfied he has done his job by notifying the Met through Arnall. What will you do with the girl?'

'I'll decide that when I hear what Steiner's up to,' said Rohm. 'I was going to phone you later. You said you were going to get Shimada, the Japanese cop.'

'He was pulled in this morning,' said Kitamura, 'and is waiting for me at the estate. If anyone knows what Steiner's planning, it's him. I'm flying there now. Why don't you come out here and get involved in the action? When I get Steiner, I'll keep him on ice until you arrive. You can catch a plane now and someone will meet you at Narita. I'll see you at the estate.'

'I'll do that,' said Rohm without hesitation. 'I'd like to see Steiner again. I'll let you know which flight I'm on.'

Chapter 33

'There has been no passport issued to a white male of Rohm's age in the last two months,' said Bruce Weisz. He was talking to Ruth Arnall in her office at the Met. 'That goes back to when he was a free man without a care in the world except crime.'

'He must be on something,' said Arnall. 'You say there was no Rohm on any of the flights leaving South Africa that tied in with his leaving jail and being seen in London.'

'Yes,' said Weisz. 'He is then either on a British passport issued abroad or the passport of another country. Rohm sounds German or Austrian and if he's from that stock he might have returned to his real roots. I'll run checks. Perhaps you can try British passports issued in London.'

'I'll set that in motion,' said Arnall, 'but I expect quite a response. We'll then have to carry out checks and it could take a while. There are a couple of other things. I tried Kirsty Callard's mobile and home numbers two hours ago and there was no reply. I left messages on both but she has not come back to me. That's a little strange for the mobile because she'd still have it with her if she'd left the house. Did she say she was moving out?'

'She wasn't going to and I said before she didn't want a presence outside the house,' said Weisz. 'I wouldn't draw too much from it. If Rohm was going to do something he'd need more time. What else do you want to tell me?'

'I was talking to the three officers who are involved in the Steiner plan earlier,' said Arnall. 'When I mentioned Kirsty's sighting of Rohm, we all agreed that my initiating a search for him might expose the plan because of Rohm's link with Steiner. I'd prefer to wait until Steiner gets back before I do anything, but if you want to go ahead, you should go through Interpol. You might already have done that.'

'The police have informed Interpol of Rohm's escape and I've not told anyone yet about the sighting,' said Weisz. 'But wait a minute. Are you telling me that no one in the Met other than the three officers knows about your getting Steiner to go after Kitamura?'

'Yes,' said Arnall. 'There's no way I would have got authorisation.'

'Does Steiner know this?' said Weisz.

'He knows I haven't had it cleared by the commissioner but thinks my boss, Craig Holden, an assistant commissioner, is in the frame. I didn't want to put him off.'

'And it's too late now to tell him,' said Weisz. 'All I can say is that I might have gone about it the same way, and even if Steiner had known, he would still have accepted. Clearly you didn't think you'd get authorisation and that wouldn't have surprised me. The next question is why are you prepared to go it alone? I told Steiner I didn't think you were motivated purely for professional reasons.'

'Brit Enoksen's family are close friends and I knew her personally,' said Arnall. 'We met when I was skiing in Norway.'

'From what you tell me I agree with you,' said Weisz, 'and don't think you should initiate any action yourself concerning Rohm. Just don't tell anyone about this conversation. Besides you, it might stick Steiner out on a limb. If your three colleagues know I put you on to Steiner, leave it at that and let them assume what they like. I'll hold back on Kirsty's sighting until Steiner gets back, and let Interpol go about their business. I wish you luck.'

'Thank you,' said Arnall. 'I'll be in touch.'

Chapter 34

Oku-Nikko
Outside Kitamura's Estate

Steiner reached Numata at seven and went to an eating house. It had taken longer than expected getting out of Tokyo and he was glad of the peace and quiet of the old merchants' town. It would be dark when he booked in at the *ryokan*.

When Steiner reached Kamata the road forked, east to Lake Sugenuma, just inside the Nikko Reserve, and north to Oshimizu, three hours by road from Numata. He took the north fork and eight kilometres from Oshimizu he came to Lake Ozenuma. He was near the *ryokan* and soon found a sign and narrow road which led to it. He entered, confirmed his booking, and after a wash in his room, went to the bar downstairs for a drink.

There were few people in the bar and as he drank he looked at Maruyama's brief. He had been through it many times and some understanding of the area was important before he went in.

The map and layout of the estate showed a period house and buildings, including the training school, dormitory and museum. The grounds were five acres and contained traditional Japanese gardens, ponds of water with the highly prized carp and a *zen* garden. The *ryokan* was two kilometres to the south of the estate which was enclosed by a six-foot stone wall with an apex of tiles and iron gates at the entrance. The period house was 300 years old with a number of rooms, and *tatami* and wooden floors. This was where Kitamura and visitors spent their time when staying, including his mistress Akiko who spent most of her time in Tokyo. According to the brief, Kitamura was on the estate each week from late Friday afternoon to Monday morning. The next visit was tonight.

Seven kilometres by road west of Lake Ozenuma was Ozegahara, a large marsh. The marsh was two kilometres from the estate, which it bordered to the south and west. The point where the road from the *ryokan* touched the marsh was the closest to the estate. A footbridge crossed to less than 500 metres from the stone wall, providing direct access and avoiding a much longer walk round the marsh. For Steiner this was as good as it could get and the first main obstacle was to gain access to the grounds by climbing over the wall. He knew Kitamura could be anywhere, including the training centre, dormitory and museum, but at some stage he would be in the period house. He didn't want to stay in the *ryokan* for more than one night, and if he couldn't get Kitamura by tomorrow evening he would find a place in Kamata where he could rest. He then thought about the actual job of getting hold of Kitamura, and he couldn't think of any place other than when he was inside the house with him and alone. The final part of the job was leaving the area with Kitamura. This meant parking the Lexus as close as possible to the estate to minimize the time spent getting to it afterwards. A sharp exit was vital.

At ten that night Steiner left the *ryokan* and drove the seven kilometres to the Ozegahara marsh. When he came to the start of the footbridge he went back a short distance until he found a well-concealed place where he could leave the Lexus. He left the car and went to a spot from which he could scan the stone wall of the estate. He used the Nikon 12x36 binoculars he had with him and swept the glasses across all visible parts.

Steiner spent thirty minutes studying what he could see, at times changing position. He only saw one guard on the gate and he assumed they changed periodically with someone else. He decided the time had come to go in.

Chapter 35

Oku-Nikko
Inside Kitamura's Estate

When he could see no one, Steiner moved quickly to the footbridge and started to cross. There was still no one in sight and he went swiftly over the planks, nailed to posts of wood driven into the bed of the marsh. He was over the water in a couple of minutes, and when he reached the far bank, went in a crouch up to the estate's stone wall. Without delay he leapt to the top, grasped the apex of tiles and pulled himself over. He rolled across the tiles in a smooth, flat movement, and dropped into a bed of plants on the other side. He was still for a moment, carefully appraising what he could of the grounds, and it was not difficult from Maruyama's description to make out the different buildings. The period house was obvious and magnificent in design and set apart from what had to be the training centre, dormitory block and the museum. The quiet reminded him of the *zen* garden, wherever it was situated, to which Maruyama had referred.

Except for what he guessed was the dormitory, the only lights on were in the period house and he moved cautiously over the finely mown lawn to the nearest door. He peered through a window, and, without haste, opened the door. He entered, and went to a door that led to a passage. He went down it and looked for stairs that he felt would lead to some sign of life and the man he was after.

The passage had a slight bend in it and when he went past it he saw a flight of stairs leading to the floor above. There was still silence as he ascended. When he reached the first floor there was another passage and some doors randomly spaced. At the end of the passage was a large door, which he went to. There was a strip of light at the bottom and he heard voices, male and female. He turned the handle and went into the room.

Seated in sumptuous chairs in the middle of the room were three men and a Japanese woman he took to be Akiko. From photographs Steiner guessed the centre of the group was Kitamura, and, unsurprisingly, one of the men was Andrew Rohm. Steiner had seen the third man before. He was one of those with Kitamura at his hotel in London.

'Well, well,' said Rohm, 'the man we have been waiting for.' He looked at Kitamura. 'Let me introduce James Steiner, the South African agent who refuses to leave me alone. I can't stand people like that and something has to be done about him.'

'It appears he has a similar feeling for me,' said Kitamura, 'and comes all this way to my estate to see me. What are we going to do with him?'

'Where's Shimada?' said Steiner. 'Picking up a police officer in Tokyo, which I believe you did, is a criminal act. Perhaps you don't understand, but I'm sure he has something to say.' He looked at Rohm. 'You've also a lot to say, but of another kind. It is time to return to Pollsmoor Prison where you belong for committing serious crimes, including, with three others, the murder of four government cabinet ministers.' Steiner then looked at Kitamura. 'You are also wanted but for a different crime, the murder of a girl in Hyde Park London. For that I want you in Tokyo for a DNA sample to be taken and matched with one found on the blade of the murder weapon.'

'This is really becoming a joke,' said Rohm and the three men laughed. He looked at David Tate. 'You know what to do.'

With the speed of a striking snake Tate sprang at Steiner and as he closed the gap he raised his hands in preparation for the lethal blows he had delivered so effectively before. When he thought he had the advantage he went low, confidence lighting up his face, and he launched the final phase of his attack. As his feet touched the floor and his hips began to rotate, Steiner moved with lightning speed. With a look of abject contempt, he swept Tate's feet high and with the bottom of his hand struck him savagely over the heart. Tate was finished, dead before he hit the floor, and as he collapsed, Steiner went for Rohm.

But Rohm's game was not over, and he went for a semi-automatic pistol inside his belt. When he took hold and was about to draw, Steiner levelled the silenced Beretta 9mm that had suddenly appeared in his hand. He pulled the trigger twice, hitting Rohm in the chest, driving him back, a tumble weed in a desert storm. He was dead, and Kitamura was perfectly still after watching the spectacle that had taken place in front of him. Akiko was spellbound, glued to the floor, not daring to move.

'Where's Shimada,' said Steiner to Akiko, the weapon hanging in his hand.

'Next door,' whispered Akiko. 'They have beaten him.'

'Take me to him,' said Steiner, 'and I want Kitamura with us.' He waved the pistol towards the door.

With Akiko leading and Kitamura following, they went down the passage and into the room next door. Shimada was in a chair, tied in an upright position with a nylon cord. He could barely move and gave a brief smile of hope when he saw Steiner.

'Cut him loose,' said Steiner to Kitamura, 'and take us to the nearest car in the yard. You will be driving.'

'You won't get away with this,' said Kitamura. 'I have some very close friends.' He cut Shimada loose.

Steiner poked him with the gun. 'Keep going, I don't want to be here longer than I can help.'

Kitamura led the way downstairs and through the rear door Steiner had used into the yard. There was a car parked round the corner at the side of the house.

Steiner opened the doors and they got in, Shimada in the front with Kitamura reluctantly behind the wheel. 'Drive to the gate and get the guard to open it,' said Steiner. 'Remember, Shimada is Japanese and speaks the language fluently. Any nonsense and I'll gun you down.'

Kitamura drove to the gate and gave the guard instructions. He clearly recognised his boss. The gate was opened and Kitamura drove through.

'Follow the road to the *ryokan*,' said Steiner. 'I'm sure you know where it is.' There was nothing he needed in the Lexus and he had decided to leave it where he had parked it.

When they reached the *ryokan*, Steiner addressed Shimada. 'Unless someone at the estate finds Rohm and Tate, there will be nothing for anyone to get excited about. We'll carry on to Tokyo and I want you to phone Maruyama and ask him to have the medical skills and DNA sample sent by Ruth Arnall available. I'll phone her when we reach Tokyo. My mobile is on the table in my room.'

They reached Tokyo a few hours later and contacted Maruyama. The sample sent by Ruth Arnall formed a perfect match with a sample taken from Kitamura. Steiner phoned Arnall in London and told her what had taken place.

'The samples are a perfect match,' said Steiner. 'What do you want me to do?'

'The Learjet will soon be at Narita,' said Arnall. 'I'll meet you in London. Kirsty phoned me after a man Moran locked her up in a private house in London and she escaped. I'll ring her.'

'Before we meet there is something that will interest you,' said Steiner. 'You'll remember the opposition sometimes appeared to be a step ahead, and we didn't know who was supplying them with information. On the way to Tokyo I asked Kitamura and, for whatever reason, he said: 'Assistant Commissioner Craig Holden with Detective Chief Superintendent Clive Dance inside'. It's a small world.'

'Thank you James, I couldn't have done it without you.'